"Okay," Tom said. "Let's give this scene a try."

"All right," Jody agreed, sitting down next to him.

Jody knew that she should be concentrating on the scene, but as Tom began reading his part of the script, she found her eyes were glued on him instead. He was handsome, Jody thought, in a relaxed, outdoorsy way. His straight, dark hair contrasted nicely with his fair skin and blue eyes. And there was a resonance of confidence and strength in his voice.

Just before it was Jody's turn to read, Tom moved a bit closer. As if his confidence was contagious, Jody started reading and found her stage fright suddenly gone. But her heart began to pound as the dialogue became more romantic.

Tom seemed to know the words by heart. He didn't look at the script but stared straight into her eyes as he told her he loved her.

"I love you, too," Jody answered, and instantly felt herself blush. It was only dialogue, but it had been so easy to say. It had felt so real.

Bantam Sweet Dreams Romances
Ask your bookseller for the books you have missed

This Time For Real

Susan Gorman

BANTAM BOOKS
TORONTO · NEW YORK · LONDON · SYDNEY · AUCKLAND

RL 6, IL age 11 and up

THIS TIME FOR REAL
A Bantam Book / June 1989

Cover photo by Pat Hill

ISBN 0-553-27175-X

Published simultaneously in the United States and Canada

*Bantam Books are published by Bantam Books, a division of
Bantam Doubleday Dell Publishing Group, Inc. Its trademark,
consisting of the words "Bantam Books" and the portrayal of a
rooster, is Registered in U.S. Patent and Trademark Office and in
other countries. Marca Registrada, Bantam Books, Inc., 666 Fifth
Avenue, New York, New York 10103.*

*Reproduced, printed and bound in Great Britain by
Hazell Watson & Viney Limited
Member of BPCC Limited
Aylesbury, Bucks, England*

To Patti Hyland Schaumberg, whose continual help, love, and guidance show me that there are always challenges worth conquering.

Chapter One

Thwack! It sounded as though a firecracker had just gone off in Jody's ear. She staggered back to catch her balance. Her head rang, and she felt her vision blur a little. Her whole face stung, and her knees buckled as a low, garbled-sounding voice called out to her, "Are you all right?"

Jody shook her head quickly and blinked her blue eyes. She leaned her back against the brick wall and buried her head in her hands. *Don't cry*, she thought to herself. *Whatever you do, don't cry.*

"Are you all right?" the voice repeated.

"Wha—" was all Jody could muster.

"I guess that's what they call a wild pitch. But I didn't mean to hit you." He looked at her carefully. "I'd better get you inside."

Jody felt a strong arm around her waist. She couldn't seem to make out who he was. He had sandy brown hair, but his coat collar was blocking his face. There was something familiar about his navy down parka and green ski hat, though. "Green ski hat," Jody murmured.

"Yeah, green ski hat. Man, I must've thrown that snowball harder than I thought," he said as he opened the glass doors of Edgeworth High.

Inside the cafeteria the warm air wrapped around Jody like a cozy blanket, and she felt the strength return to her legs.

"You'd better sit down," he continued, helping her to sit in a cafeteria chair. "School's out, but you want me to try to find the nurse, anyway?"

Just as Jody was beginning to feel like her old self again, she remembered where she had seen that ski hat a million times before. On top of Jeff Reynolds's head. It was like a trademark of his. Coca-Cola had its red-and-white can, and Jeff Reynolds was never seen without his famous green ski hat.

"Jeff Reynolds!" Jody cried, feeling woozy again, but for a different reason this time.

"Yeah, yeah, I'm Jeff. Look, I didn't realize the snow was so wet, or that I'd thrown it so hard. I didn't even see you."

Jody didn't say a word; she just stared at his

2

soft brown eyes and long eyelashes. *Why were long eyelashes always wasted on guys?* she wondered. *I'd give my right arm to have those lashes.*

"Like I said, it was a wild pitch."

"I'm fine, really I'm okay. I was just stunned for a second," she said nervously.

"You sure?" Jeff said, kneeling by her side. "I really clobbered you out there."

Jody raised her hand to the right side of her head. It felt cold and wet, but at least it was in one piece.

"I think everything's still here. Maybe it knocked some sense into me, or if I'm really lucky, at least a better understanding of geometry."

"Maybe you should take a couple of potshots at me," Jeff said teasingly. "I could use the extra help in biology." His smile broadened, and he laughed. "Anyway, I'm really sorry I plastered you—uh, uh, I don't know your name."

"Jody—Jody Bauer."

"Do I know you from someplace? You look kind of familiar."

Jody shrugged. "I'm in your history and biology classes."

"Oh, so you're a junior, too," he said, standing.

"Uh, no. I'm just a sophomore. I've taken a lot of sciences and stuff, though. . . ." her voice trailed off uncomfortably. Although Jeff was on the varsity football and baseball teams, he probably wasn't taking accelerated classes.

"Oh, well, what were you doing outside in the cold, anyway?"

"I was supposed to meet my friend Marlie, Marlie Anderson. We usually walk home together, but she's late." Jody glanced at her watch and looked over her shoulder.

"Yeah, I know Marlie," Jeff said, looking around as well. "She's real cute, great smile."

"Yeah, she is," Jody admitted while trying to hide her braces.

"Well, Laura—my girlfriend—was supposed to meet me, too, so if you feel up to it we could look for them together."

"Great," Jody said, practically jumping to her feet.

"You're a cheerleader, aren't you?" Jeff asked as they started down the first hallway.

"I wish," Jody grunted. "I tried out but I didn't make it. I made it past the panel, but the student body didn't vote for me." Since Edgeworth was a relatively small school, those trying out for cheerleading were first judged for skill in front of a panel of teachers. Then ten were selected to try out and be voted on by the student body. Six were chosen, and Jody had been devastated not to have been one of them.

"Ah, it's all a popularity contest, anyway," Jeff said offhandedly. "But that's where I remember you from. I thought you were real good, too. I voted for you."

"Really?" Jody couldn't believe what she was hearing.

"Sure. You should try out again next year. I bet you make it. Sophomores rarely win, anyway."

"Really," Jody repeated as they rounded the corner into the commons area. She was thrilled to think that Jeff Reynolds had noticed her, let alone voted for her. By now she wasn't looking for Marlie at all. In fact, she hoped they wouldn't find either of the girls, so she and Jeff could keep walking the halls alone. Jody tried to fluff up her matted long, blond hair where the snowball had hit it. She couldn't believe she was walking with Jeff Reynolds, the most gorgeous hunk in Edgeworth High. Maybe she had been knocked unconscious by the snowball, and this was all a dream.

"No luck here." Jeff broke the silence. "Let's go this way."

Jody didn't care if it was a dream or not, she was going to enjoy it. It felt great just to stand next to Jeff. All five foot seven inches of her. That was something she liked about high school; guys like Jeff were tall and muscular. For the first time in her life, she could wear high heels and not feel like the Empire State Building. Now she understood what it must be like to date an upperclassman.

Their search led them down two more hallways. They passed a couple holding hands and a senior boy who had his arm around a girl in Jody's class. They were almost out of places to look, when they passed a couple stealing a kiss behind the lockers.

"Looks like fun," Jeff said, mischievously raising his eyebrows.

"Yeah," Jody answered, giggling uncontrollably. Immediately she covered her mouth to muffle the sound and hide her braces. *What a dumb thing to say. I can't believe I laughed like that. How uncool.* Her mind raced. *How would I know if kissing was fun or not? Nobody's ever tried to kiss a metal mouth!*

They checked the gym, and an awkward silence grew as they walked toward the auditorium where a group of students had gathered around the front doors.

"Looks like something's going on over there," Jeff said as he picked up his pace. "Maybe they've seen the girls."

"Right," Jody answered a little disappointed. She was glad to have the sound barrier broken, but she had been hoping they could walk alone longer. "In fact, I think I see Marlie," she added, keeping up with Jeff. She knew it was silly, but she wanted the other girls to see them walk up together.

A group of students was gathered around a large white poster with green lettering on it. From where she stood the only word Jody could make out was Auditions. Jeff recognized Laura Fielding and headed in her direction. Jody saw Marlie's tweed jacket and approached her.

"What's going on? I waited out front in the cold for over fifteen minutes."

"Sorry," Marlie answered with a shrug. "I got wrapped up in this audition thing. Here, read it," she said pushing Jody to the front of the group. "You'd be perfect for this." Jody read the information:

Edgeworth High will be producing the musical *Finian's Rainbow*, in conjunction with Bradford High School. Singing, acting, and dancing auditions will be held Friday, January 6 at Bradford beginning at 3:00 P.M. Bring in a short song or dance, and be prepared to read from the script.

Available Roles: There are three male singing leads: Woody, the hero; Finian, the heroine's father; and Og, the mischievous leprechaun who is losing his magical powers. Also the mayor and the sheriff are male

7

roles. The female leads include Sharon, the romantic heroine, and Susan the Silent, Woody's mute sister who dances her conversations. Other roles are for dancers and singers.

Jody stood quietly for a moment, thinking about the roles. Auditions were this Friday? That was only four days away! Her expression slowly changed to a smile and then as she turned to face Marlie it widened to a real grin. "Sounds exciting."

"I thought you might think so," Marlie said, flashing her straight, white, perfectly shaped teeth. "You'd be perfect for this, Jody. You've been taking ballet for over five years, and you're the best dancer in Miss Hawkins's Ballet School."

"Well, what about you?" Jody asked.

"I will if you will," Marlie said, daring her.

"You'll both have to pass *my* dance audition first," Laura Fielding interrupted, flipping back her jet black hair.

"*Your* dance audition?" Marlie repeated.

"Mrs. French, the director for the show, has asked me to choreograph the dance numbers. Since I was the lead dancer in last year's production, I was the logical choice."

"What kind of dancers are you looking for?" Jody asked eagerly.

"If I told you," Laura answered with exaggerated patience, "that would be cheating. All I can say is that there are a lot of girls who were in the show last year who are trying out again. They have the necessary experience."

"Is there anything you *can* tell us?" Jody asked, beginning to feel annoyed.

"Well, you should try to look your absolute best," Laura said. "Be poised, show personality, and whatever you do, smile."

Jody took her hands out of her coat pockets, straightened her scarf, and ran her fingers through her hair. She felt like a cadet on the first day at West Point.

"The characters in the show are either poor or Irish," Laura explained as if she were holding court. "So you might want to keep that in mind. Now, we realize that they wouldn't have worn braces or had pierced ears, but things like that won't be held against you."

Jody felt as if everyone's eyes had suddenly focused on her, and she knew her face was bright crimson. She relaxed her military posture and quickly covered her mouth. *Why did Laura have to mention braces?* she thought miserably. More than two years of wearing them had already put a major roadblock in her social life. She didn't need a reminder.

"One last thing," Laura added. "You'll need to bring your own sheet music, record, or cassette."

By now almost everyone was drifting away. Laura was finishing some last-minute details with a few of the kids, so Jody wandered over to Jeff. "Are you planning on auditioning?" Jody asked shyly.

"I don't know." Jeff shrugged casually. "Maybe if they ask me."

"You sing great in choir class, you'd be a shoo-in," Marlie said.

"Well, the shows are pretty popular around here," Jeff said. "I had the lead last year. How about you, Jody. Are you going to audition?"

"I think so," Jody said, carefully smiling so her braces wouldn't show. "As long as the student body isn't voting on it, I'll probably give it a shot. Maybe I'll see you there."

"Oh, he'll be there," Laura said, joining them and slipping her arm into Jeff's, "if I have to drag him there myself. Sorry I kept you waiting," she continued, tugging him away from Jody and closer to the exit door. "But I promised Mrs. French that I'd post the announcement. I hope you weren't too bored."

"Nah, I was just throwing snowballs with some of the guys. . . ." Jeff's voice trailed off as they went down the hall.

Jody watched them walk off, arm in arm. "I guess they're a couple, huh?"

"Only since homecoming, dummy," Marlie

said, picking her books up off the floor. "And since when did you get so chummy with Jeff Reynolds?"

"Just today. He knocked me over with a snowball."

"Lucky you," said Marlie, following Jody to the exit. "How'd it happen?"

Jody was barely listening to Marlie; she had other things on her mind. A plan—a plan that would solve all her problems. If everything worked out the way she hoped, Jody would be cast in the play opposite Jeff, they would fall in love, start dating—and she'd be sure to get her first real kiss.

Chapter Two

Jody pushed open the school door, and a blast of cold air and swirling snow snapped her back to reality.

"It's really coming down hard," Marlie shouted over the slamming door. "If it keeps up like this, maybe they'll cancel school tomorrow."

"That would be great, then we could practice for our auditions."

"I hope we have a chance at this," Marlie said glumly. "All those friends of Laura's are going to be tough to beat."

"We'll just have to be that much better," Jody stated with determination as they headed down the first sloping hill to go home.

"The announcement sheet said that there was only one female lead dancer."

"Right, she's Susan the Silent who can't talk, so she dances her conversations."

"Sounds weird," Marlie said.

"Sounds great to me. If she can't talk, then she doesn't have to sing, either. At least you can sing."

"Not well enough to do the lead. The poster said there are chorus dancers. That's for me."

"Hey, maybe Miss Hawkins will let us use her dance studio to practice in. I bet she'd even help us if we ask her to."

"Perfect!" exclaimed Marlie. "Oh, I hope we get cast. You know," she said, grabbing Jody's elbow, "this could even be a better way to meet guys than working on the float or being a cheerleader."

Jody grinned at her friend. "How do you figure that?"

"Well, cheerleaders just yell for the guys at the games. They don't actually talk to them, and they practice by themselves."

"Mmmm," Jody agreed, starting to see the light.

"And when we worked on the homecoming float, it was the girls who showed up every night, not the guys."

"True," Jody admitted.

"So, *everyone* in the cast, guys included, will have to be at all the rehearsals."

"You're boy crazy," Jody announced as they approached the crest of the first hill.

Marlie looked skeptical. "And you're not?"

"Well, I hate to think I'm that desperate. I refuse to be like Cheryl Weber. She's so preoccupied with boys that she's lost interest in everything else. I refuse to lose my personality because of any boy," Jody vowed.

"Jeff Reynolds included?"

"Jeff Reynolds included. If I get cast in this show, I'll work hard, make new friends, and maybe even find my niche at school. But I will definitely not do it to meet boys."

"All right, all right," Marlie said. "I believe you."

"On the other hand," Jody said, looking out of the corner of her eye, "if we happen to meet a couple of terrific guys, so be it." The girls laughed and turned down Marlie's street. "I never thought I'd fit in at Edgeworth," Jody confided. "But if I could be cast in the show, I just might be on my way."

Jody had lived in Greeley, Colorado, since she was five. It was a great place to grow up. A quiet college town, big enough to keep things changing, but small enough for Jody to know most of her neighbors. So it was a shock when the past spring her parents had moved to the other side of town.

Her older brothers, Bud and Paul, were in their sophomore and junior years when they had to transfer to Edgeworth from Bradford. But the April move didn't seem to upset the boys the way it had Jody, who had been a freshman at the time.

"When we moved out here last year," Jody said, "I thought I'd never make any new friends or get involved in school."

"Well, it was hard when you only had two and a half months before school ended," Marlie said. "I'm glad I didn't have to make a whole new group of friends like that."

"Yeah, well I'd be a basket case if it weren't for you. If you hadn't come into my ballet class last summer, I'd still be moping around our house," said Jody, pulling Marlie's knit hat over her eyes.

"Thanks," Marlie said sarcastically. She pulled her hat off and ran a hand through her short blond hair. "You must miss your old friends, though."

"Sure," Jody admitted. "But I want to be accepted in Edgeworth. Becoming a cheerleader would have clinched it."

"It wasn't meant to be," Marlie said. "Besides that would have been too easy."

Jody moaned. "I know, 'challenge builds character.' Have you been talking to my mother? You sure sound like her."

"I'll never tell," Marlie cried, scooping up a

handful of snow and putting it down Jody's coat.

"You creep!" muttered Jody. "See if I tell you what Jeff Reynolds said about you."

"What?"

"No way." Jody was still shaking the snow out of her coat.

"Come on, please."

"All right." Jody gave in reluctantly. "He said you were cute."

"He didn't really?"

Marlie came to a stop at the bottom of her driveway.

"Would I lie to you?"

"Yes, but tell me more when you call tonight, okay?" Marlie's voice drifted away as she walked to her back door.

"I'll call Miss Hawkins about the studio," Jody shouted as she started down the last two blocks toward home.

Jody walked up the driveway of her family's two-story, colonial house, kicked off her snowy shoes at the back door, and went inside, searching for a snack. She scavenged through the cookie jar but opted for a Granny Smith apple. *If I'm going to look my best at the auditions on Friday I'd better start now,* she thought.

The house was unusually quiet for a Monday afternoon, so Jody decided to take full advantage of the living room stereo. She thumbed through the family collection of albums and cassettes, and sure enough there was a record of *Finian's Rainbow*.

"What luck," Jody said, glancing at the list of songs. Her eye caught the title, "The Rain Dance Ballet," so she read the jacket for the description:

"The Rain Dance Ballet" is a dramatic dance number for Susan the Silent. She's watched her brother kiss Sharon, the Irish girl, and her own feelings for Og, the leprechaun, are growing. During the rainstorm she dances her emotions. In essence, this is Susan's solo about a girl changing into a woman.

"Perfect," Jody said, placing the record on the turntable. The music began and she listened, standing perfectly still. She was already thinking of steps and combinations. She played the song three times, trying to feel the mood of the piece. Finally, she began to move. *This feels great*, she thought, turning an arabesque. She started the song again and worked on putting a combination together. She was concentrating so hard that she didn't notice both of her older brothers watching her. As she finished a turn they burst into wild laughter.

"Very funny," Jody said, flicking off the music. "I don't make fun of your stupid wrestling moves, so I'd appreciate it if you'd keep your comments to yourself about my dancing."

"What are you doing, anyway?" Bud asked, still laughing. "You're not trying out for cheerleading again, are you?"

"I know what it is," Paul said. "You're going to try out for that ridiculous play at school, aren't you?"

"And what if I am?" Jody demanded.

"This could be worse than having to sit through that dumb dance recital last spring," Bud said, flapping his arms like a swan.

"You don't have to come," Jody said, marching past them. "Besides, I'm not in the show yet."

Paul followed her, looking concerned. "You're not going to sing, are you?"

"Maybe you'll be cast in one of the men's roles," Bud called helpfully.

"Yeah, because no decent guy would be caught dead doing a sissy musical," Paul shouted.

Jody stormed through the dining room, picked up her books from the kitchen table, and headed upstairs. She could still hear Bud and Paul laughing as she slammed her bedroom door. A few years before she would have run to her mom for protection. Now she was just angry that she'd let them get her riled. "Ugh, brothers!" she said aloud, dropping her books on the desk. There was a soft knock on the door, followed by a blond head poking its way in.

"Are you okay?" her younger brother, Jack, asked.

"Sure, Jack-o." Jody halfheartedly smiled. "Thanks."

"I like the way you dance," he assured her before closing the door and scampering back down the hall.

Jody plopped down on her bed. *I don't care what they say about my dancing,* she thought, *just please make sure Jeff auditions. My whole plan will be spoiled if he doesn't.*

As if to drown out her own thoughts, Jody clicked on the radio. The music was suddenly interrupted by a special announcement: "Because of the increasing amount of snowfall and hazardous road conditions, district six schools will be closed tomorrow." Jody lay back and smiled.

Jody slid open the glass doors of Miss Hawkins's Ballet School. She was so glad Miss Hawkins had agreed to help her and Marlie put their audition material together. The room was a renovated garage, which worked perfectly as a dance studio. A mirror covered one wall, and across from it was a long barre, where the students began each class. In one corner there was a large record collection next to the stereo; a built-in bench took up the rest of the wall, and there was a small changing room just beyond.

"Good morning, Jody," Miss Hawkins said, standing in the doorway by the record player. "Change into your dance clothes, and I'll come back to help you. I still have a few more mothers to call to cancel today's classes." She disappeared, closing the door, leaving Jody and Marlie together.

Marlie, who had already changed, looked up from a stretch. "Isn't this a great way to spend a Tuesday?"

"Sure beats Mr. Freeman's history class," Jody agreed, ducking into the changing room.

"I came over early to listen to Miss Hawkins's record of the show. She's been helping me," Marlie said, raising her voice so Jody would hear. "I think I'm going to do a jig for my audition. Hurry up and tell me what you think so far."

When Jody came out Marlie placed the needle on the record and began prancing in one place. Her feet lightly bounced off the floor in rhythm with the music. "Miss Hawkins says when you do an Irish jig, you don't use your arms. Isn't that wild?"

"You're kidding," Jody said, pulling on her pink leg warmers and shoes.

Marlie collapsed to the floor. "All this bouncing around is exhausting. Your turn to show me your dance so far."

"Yes," their teacher said, gracefully entering the studio. "Let's see Jody's audition piece."

"Well, I haven't finished it yet," Jody admitted.

"First lesson about auditioning," Miss Hawkins said, positioning Jody in the center of the room. "Never apologize. Even if you are dancing on a broken leg. You don't want to put negative thoughts in the director's head."

Jody and Marlie exchanged glances and nodded as if to make a mental note.

"Now close your eyes," Miss Hawkins continued, starting the record player. "See yourself dancing. Watch your arms extend and your toes point. Feel the music, and let your spirit carry you across the floor. You know the steps and the technique, now begin."

Jody stood motionless while the introduction played. As she began the first combination she felt lighter, somehow. Her legs seemed solid, and her turns were fluid and strong. At that moment Jody knew what it was like to be a real dancer. *Keep your concentration*, she thought, but as she finished a grand jeté her heart sank. Out the window, she spied Laura Fielding walking toward the studio.

"Laura," Jody cried, falling out of her spin.

"Where?" Marlie asked, rushing over and peeking through the curtains.

"Outside, I could've sworn I saw her walking this way."

Marlie shook her head. "There's nobody out there, not even a snowman. Laura's got you paranoid. You were doing great until you thought you saw her."

"I'm sure it was Laura," Jody said stubbornly.

"Did you girls come to dance or tell ghost stories?" Miss Hawkins demanded, her dark eyes staring at them.

"To dance," the girls said together.

"Then come to the barre and do so."

Jody looked out the window one last time. She was sure Laura must be hiding in the bushes.

"Feet in first position, *round de jambe*. One . . ." Miss Hawkins's voice began a familiar patter.

"What is it with you and Laura?" Marlie whispered from behind.

"I don't know. She has me so nervous I see her everywhere. How am I going to be able to make it through the audition if I can't even dance when she's not around?"

"Beats me," Marlie said in hushed tones.

"Thanks a lot."

"Fifth position," Miss Hawkins called louder than usual. Obviously she was aware of their conversation.

"You'll have to block her out. Think about something more pleasant," Marlie said.

Right, Jody thought, *something or someone.* She'd think about doing the show with Jeff instead. But mostly she'd concentrate on her dancing.

Later that evening, after having dinner at Marlie's house and doing biology, Jody gathered her books and dance clothes and went home. She slowly walked inside and upstairs to her bedroom. There she dumped her things on a chair, slipped into her oversize T-shirt, and stared at herself in the mirror. "Would you cast this girl in a musical?" she asked, pointing to her reflection. "It's an okay face, not great but okay." She piled her straight, fine hair on top of her head and sucked in her cheeks, finally deciding she didn't fit the cliché of the gorgeous, blue-eyed blonde. "Go to bed," she said, dropping her hands to her side.

Jody cleared the stuffed animals and dolls from her bed and climbed under the covers. Although her body was tired, her mind was in overdrive. She tossed and turned, her head full of dance combinations and biology terms. Every few minutes she'd jump up and go through parts of her dance audition.

"What's going on in there?" Paul cried, pounding on their mutual wall.

"Go to sleep," Jody said, pounding back.

"I can't sleep with a herd of elephants running through my room!"

Jody jumped back into bed and tried to go over the steps in her head. As she started to drift off, visions of dancers flashed in her mind. She saw herself standing on a stage with garlands of flowers hung overhead. She danced so gracefully, her feet barely touched the ground. Suddenly a tall, dark figure walked over to her. They danced together. He twirled her around, lifted her over his head, and then gently lowered her to face him. He bent down to kiss her. She couldn't see who it was, but she was sure it was Jeff. Just before their lips touched, Laura stepped in. Jody stood there helplessly as Laura danced away with the tall, handsome figure.

Chapter Three

Friday, the day of the auditions, had arrived. The week had gone by quickly. Between dance class, biology, and audition practice, Jody had hardly thought of anything else, except maybe her dream and Jeff Reynolds. She stared at the large wooden doors of Bradford High. In all the ways that Edgeworth was a new and modern school, Bradford was old and traditional. Jody's mind raced with mixed emotions. She was excited and nervous about the auditions, homesick for her old school friends who went to Bradford, yet loyal to her new. So much depended on what happened that day. If the audition went well and her plans with Jeff worked out, her life would be perfect. If not, she was sure she was destined to become a high school washout.

Jody had talked to her old Bradford buddy, Rosemary, the night before and was disappointed to find out that most of her friends weren't auditioning for the show, and those that were had tried out the day before. Because there were two schools involved, different auditions had been set up for each. So, Jody would be on her own.

I wish Marlie were here, Jody thought, walking through the entrance. Marlie, she knew, was waiting for the results of her biology exam, since her father had said she could only try out for the show if she got a B or better on the test. Their biology teacher had been reluctant to grade the test on the spot, but Marlie had pleaded and he was still marking her paper when Jody left for Bradford. Praying that Marlie would get her B, Jody followed the signs and arrows directing her toward the auditorium.

"Please sign in and pick up a number before going into the auditorium," Mrs. French, the director, announced. "And fill out the information card Laura will give you."

Jody stepped in line behind a group of Laura's cheerleading friends and a boy she didn't know.

"Don't be nervous," Mrs. French said kindly as she gave Jody a number.

"I'll try not to be," Jody answered through a shaky smile.

"You're one of the last ones to audition, number seventy-two, so you'll have some time to relax. But don't forget to get an information card from Laura."

"I told you exactly what we're looking for. Now, just do it," Laura tried to whisper to one of her friends.

"*If I told you, that would be cheating.*" Laura's line rang through Jody's memory. "Excuse me, Laura," Jody interrupted, "I need to get an information card from you.

"Oh, yeah, sure, here," Laura said handing Jody a blank index card.

"What am I supposed to put on it?"

Laura paused and placed her hands on her hips. "Your name, school, experience."

"Experience?" Jody questioned.

"You know, like have you ever done a play before."

"Oh. No, I haven't," Jody answered quietly, "but I've done dance recitals."

"Well, if that's all you have, you better put that down, as well as what kind of dance and how many years you've taken."

"Ballet, five years."

"Put it on the card," Laura replied, walking away.

Jody didn't understand why Laura was so mean to her, but she was bound and determined to find out—eventually. That day, however, she had more important things to do.

Jody walked over to the stairway and sat on the bottom step to fill out her card.

"Number twelve," Mrs. French's voice rang through the halls.

Jody realized she couldn't stay in the stairwell until her number was called. She'd go crazy first, she was sure. Marlie wasn't around, and there was no one to talk to. Jody grasped the banister and walked slowly upstairs. The sounds of voices singing and talking faded with each step. The second floor hallway was quiet, and the coolness and solitude seemed to calm her. The winter sun was waning, so the light created long shadows through the glass windows. Jody let her dance bag slide off her shoulder and thud on the floor. "Practice," she said in a whisper. She began performing her routine. The rhythms of her feet echoed through the halls like a metronome keeping time. She turned, kicked, and smiled, playing to an audience of lockers. And as she completed her final bow, the silence was broken by applause.

"Bravo, Bravo," cried the voice at the end of the hall.

"Oh, no!" Jody gasped, scrambling to pick up

her dance bag. Flinging it over her shoulder, she darted to the nearest doorway. She could still hear herself breathing as she swung open the creaky, wooden door of the girls' bathroom. She stood motionless, her back against the cool, green tile, her heart pounding like a drum. She had only caught a glimpse of her fan, but he was tall and had dark hair. *Like the guy in my dream*, she thought, facing the walls of her sanctuary. *He must think I'm a complete idiot, dancing around the halls. But at least he applauded, instead of laughing*, she reasoned. She ran cold water over a paper towel and dabbed at her forehead. *He was tall and broad shouldered*, Jody remembered. *And it looked like he was wearing a letter jacket. It would be just my luck to have someone see me acting weird.*

She crossed to the door and quietly opened it a crack. Outside she could hear the sounds of heels clicking along the floor, so she quickly closed the door and returned to her refuge. *I'll get ready in here.* Hurriedly, she pulled out the contents of her bag and scattered them on the floor.

After trying on dozens of dance clothes at home, she'd chosen a turquoise blue, shiny Spandex leotard. It had long sleeves and a V neckline. The cut of the material and extra piping accentuated her tiny waist, and the demi-French cut showed off her long legs. Her tights were pale pink, and her leg warmers, a lighter shade of turquoise blue, had three small pink buttons down the sides. Unfortunately, her ballet slippers were a wreck. They used to be a pretty pink, but now they resembled a mix between the bottom of a Pepto-Bismol bottle and a pair of scuffed-up sneakers. Jody pulled down her leg warmers to hide the shoes as much as possible.

After stuffing her street clothes back in her bag, she touched up her makeup. Suddenly Jody glanced at her watch. "Oh, no!" she gasped. "I've been up here for over forty minutes." She threw her makeup into her purse, shoved it into the already bulging dance bag, and dashed out of the door and down the vacant hallway. She flew down the stairs three at a time, praying she wouldn't break her neck or, worse, miss her number.

"Numbers seventy through eighty, pay attention," Mrs. French called. "Number seventy come in, and numbers seventy-one and seventy-two, please get ready."

"Jody," a familiar voice called out. "I've been looking for you all over the place. Look!" Marlie held up her biology test. "B-plus, can you believe it? I'm going to frame it!"

"That's great," Jody said, giving Marlie a hug. "I knew you'd do it. Did you tell your dad?"

"Called him from the office at school. He asked if trying out for the volleyball team might help my math grade."

"Maybe this is your lucky day," Jody said with a laugh. "Now just go in there and knock 'em dead. What's your number?"

"Number eighty-four." Marlie sighed, sitting on the step below Jody. "I'm the last one. Where are they now?"

"Number seventy-two, number seventy-two, please. Last call for seventy-two," Mrs. French called from the auditorium door. "Oh, my gosh. That's me," Jody cried. "I got so wrapped up. I'm here, seventy-two is coming!" she shouted.

"Don't forget your dance bag," Marlie added. "Good luck!"

Jody clutched her bag, unzipped the top, reached for her tape, and dashed to the auditorium door. She was going at a gallop when she pushed open the door and ran full steam into number seventy-one leaving his audition. They both hung on to each other to keep from falling, but his sheet music and Jody's open dance bag became casualties.

"I'm sorry," he said. "I didn't see you coming."

"I didn't hear them call my number, and when I did I thought they'd pass me up if I didn't hurry," Jody explained frantically. "It's so dark in the auditorium, I think I went blind coming in."

"Just relax. We'll get all your stuff together, and you'll be fine," the stranger assured her.

"That's easy for you to say. You've finished auditioning, but I've still got to face the panel and lovely Laura."

"Who?"

"Love— never mind." Jody fished around in the darkness and found her sneaker. "I think I've got everything. I'm sorry about crashing into you. I'm just a little nervous."

"That's okay, just take a deep breath and you'll dance great. I'll double-check to see if we found everything. You go ahead."

"Thanks," Jody whispered. *How did he know I was going to dance? Must be the leotard*, she thought, stuffing her sweater back in the bag.

Onstage the lights were so bright that Jody couldn't even see the panel, but she could hear them. Jody tried to make out the faces, but deep down inside she was glad that she couldn't see anyone staring at her.

"Please hand your information card to Laura, and then you may start your audition," Mrs. French said. Jody marched to the edge of the stage where Laura snatched her card. Then she reached into the front pocket of her dance bag for the cassette of *Finian's Rainbow* that she had taped from the record the night before. She fumbled briefly, but the tape wasn't there. She tried the two side pockets, and as the sweat started to bead up on her forehead she began frantically dumping everything on the stage floor. "I know it's here. I know it's here," Jody mumbled to herself.

"Is this part of your routine?" Mrs. French called.

Jody was too scared to speak, so she mimed a few gestures and bounded off the stage to where the bag had fallen. In the shadows at the back of the auditorium, the boy she crashed into handed her the tape.

"It was under the chair, and here's another sneaker. Good luck."

"Thanks," Jody muttered before darting back on the stage.

Without saying a word, Jody held up her cassette for the panel to see.

"I'm sorry, Jody," Mrs. French said. "We announced earlier that the cassette player isn't working. You'll have to dance without music or see if one of the other kids has one."

All the expression disappeared from Jody's face. It wasn't going at all as she had planned it. Her feet felt glued to the stage and her face was terror stricken.

"I've got one in my locker," the boy called from the back of the auditorium. "I'll be back in a flash." Jody could hardly believe this guy was coming to her rescue again. She felt herself relax a little, and the stage seemed to loosen its grip on her feet so she decided to do a few warm-up stretches. The time seemed to pass so slowly. She hoped she wouldn't die before the next minute was up.

"Maybe we should go on to the next audition," Laura's voice pierced through the wall of light. *No*, Jody shook her head back and forth. She was still too nervous to speak. She could feel her knees start to shake.

"It's all right, Jody," Mrs. French called. "We can wait a few more minutes."

"Here it is, Mrs. French," the boy called, jumping on the front of the stage. "I'll plug it in over by the piano. All you have to do is punch Play," he whispered to Jody, who had joined him.

What seemed like an eternity later, Jody was dancing her routine. The music flowed through her body. Each expressive movement was better than the last. Her concentration was solid and her rhythm precise. Jody was bitten by the "stage bug," and the dance went better than ever. She felt great when she heard applause from the panel.

"That was very nice, Jody. Well worth waiting

for," Mrs. French called. "Would you like to sing for us as well?" The old fear sank back into Jody's body as she shook her head no.

"All right, then we'd like to hear you read something from the script. Laura, give Jody a script and have her read with Jeff or one of the others," Mrs. French went on.

Jody smiled agreeably, gathered her dance bag paraphernalia, and walked off the stage. Nothing could spoil the terrific mood she was in now—nothing except Laura.

"Here's the script," Laura said sharply as they left the auditorium. "You'll have a few minutes to rehearse out here before we call you in."

"A few minutes?" Jody echoed.

"It's a romantic scene between Og and Susan the Silent," Laura stated. "After she gets her voice back, of course."

"Great," Jody said, still a little out of breath from the dancing.

Laura looked at her coldly. "That was an interesting act you just did for your audition."

"Act?"

"Yeah, act. Forgetting your tape, pretending that you couldn't talk."

Jody stared at Laura, amazed. She couldn't believe what she was hearing.

"A clever trick to get you the part of Susan

the Silent," Laura went on. "There's just one problem. It didn't work. I saw right through it."

"That was not a trick," Jody said indignantly, "I was scared stiff in there."

"Well, now comes the tough part." Laura handed her the script. "You'll have to prove to the director you can act. You may be able to look good doing your own dance routine, but reading from a script you've never seen before is the true test of an actress."

Jody stared blankly at the typewritten pages in front of her. It all seemed like a dream turned nightmare. She could almost feel the confidence drain from her body. She'd been so busy working on her dance audition, she never even thought about having to do anything else.

"Now let's find your partner," Laura said, ignoring Jody's dismayed expression.

Jeff will help me, Jody thought trying to quell a rising wave of panic. *Yes, reading with Jeff will make it easier. He'll be confident. He had the lead last year, he'll give me some acting tips. Besides it won't be acting if I'm supposed to be in love with him.*

"There's Jeff over there," Jody said, pointing to the far end of the hallway.

"Oh, you're not with Jeff," Laura assured her.

"But Mrs. French said," Jody began.

"I know what Mrs. French said."

"She said Jeff Reynolds."

"She said Jeff or one of the others who had already sung."

"But I thought!"

Laura's smile was venomous. "You thought wrong. Mrs. French trusts me to match up people of the same caliber of talent, and since you're in cahoots with one of the others you might as well finish your 'act' with him."

"Cahoots? What are you talking about?"

"You know who I mean. It won't do you any good to play dumb."

"I really don't know what you're talking about."

"Right, why else would that guy from Bradford be auditioning on Edgeworth's day?"

"Laura!" Jody began.

"Here." Laura tapped the boy on the shoulder. "Since you two are so chummy, you'll read together. You have about five minutes before we call you."

"Great." Jody sighed, still half-dazed. She watched Laura storm off in Jeff's direction.

"So we meet again," the tall, dark-haired boy from Bradford said, taking his hands out of his pockets.

"Thanks for helping me before," Jody said, taking a good look at him for the first time. "I don't know what I would have done if you hadn't had a tape player."

"I was glad to help," he replied. His blue eyes sparkled, and a slight dimple appeared on the left side of his face when he smiled.

"So, I guess we're supposed to read this scene together."

"Yeah, I guess so."

"Well, we might as well dive in," Jody said, suddenly feeling self-conscious in front of this stranger.

"Right," the boy said, extending his hand. "By the way, I'm Tom. Tom Arnold."

"Jody Bauer," she said, returning his firm handshake. Jody's eyes widened as she felt a tingling sensation rush through her arm. It was only a handshake, but it seemed electric. She saw that Tom wore a Bradford class ring with the year engraved on the side. *He's a sophomore, too*, she realized. "You go to Bradford, don't you?" Jody broke the trance, and they simultaneously released their grasp. "Why didn't you audition yesterday?"

"I couldn't. I had a dentist's appointment, so Mrs. French was nice enough to let me try out with you guys from Edgeworth."

"I was auditioning for the dancer's role. I never thought I'd have to act," Jody said, nervously clasping her hands together; she could still feel his touch.

Tom smiled. "There's nothing to be scared

of," he said gently. "It's like reading out loud in front of your English class."

"Maybe you're right."

"Sure I am." Tom headed toward the stairway. "Let's sit down and give this scene a try."

"All right," Jody agreed, sitting on the steps and gazing up at him.

Tom began reading his part of the script. Jody knew she should be concentrating on the scene, but her eyes were glued on Tom instead. He was handsome, Jody thought, in a relaxed, outdoorsy way. His straight, dark hair contrasted with his fair skin and blue eyes. And there was a resonance of confidence and strength in his voice.

Just before it was Jody's turn to begin reading, Tom eased down on the step so that they were sitting close. It was as if his confidence was contagious. Jody started reading, her stage fright suddenly gone. But her heart began to pound as the dialogue became more romantic.

Tom seemed to know the words by heart. He didn't look at the script but stared straight into her eyes as he told her that he loved her.

"I love you, too," Jody answered and instantly felt herself blush. It was only dialogue, but it had been so easy to say. It had felt so real. Jody shook her head, as if to wake herself from a trance.

41

"Nice going," Tom said as Laura signaled to them from the auditorium. "You just may be a natural."

"Molly Ringwald, watch out," Jody joked.

"Meryl Streep is more like it," Tom said. "Take my word for it. You're going to knock them out of their seats."

"Right," Jody said with a laugh. But for the first time that day, she believed that she could.

Chapter Four

"It's been a whole week," Jody said, slamming her locker door shut. "What could be taking them so long? It's driving me crazy."

"I hadn't noticed." Marlie said sarcastically, leaning back against the next locker. "You've been bonkers since the auditions."

"I can't help it. My whole future depends on getting cast in this show."

"Well, worrying about it won't make it happen any faster. Come on." Marlie tugged on the sleeve of Jody's oversize peach sweatshirt. "We're going to be late for psychology class."

"If I just knew when they were going to tell us, then I could put my emotions on hold for a while."

"Dream on," Marlie said, rolling her eyes.

"Well, I could try."

"I want to know, too, but you don't see me acting like some possessed creature. I believe in the theory of a watched pot never boils."

"You know you're scaring me, Marlie," Jody said, stopping short. "You're sounding more and more like my mother every day. Come on, let's walk past Mrs. French's room. Maybe the list is up."

"We've gone by that room eight times today. There's a rut in the floor from our lockers to her door." Marlie shifted her books on her hip. "Besides, we're late for psych class already, and you know what an ogre Mr. Miles is about that."

"We'll walk by fast," said Jody, starting to jog.

"We'll check after class on our way to lunch," Marlie said firmly. "Hey"—she pointed down the hall—"isn't that Jeff?"

"Where?" Jody strained her neck. "I don't see him."

"Down by Mr. Miles's door. Come on."

Jody shifted into fifth gear, and the girls maneuvered through the crowds toward their classroom.

"I didn't see Jeff out there," Jody said, sliding into her seat as the bell rang.

"He wasn't. I just couldn't think of a faster way to get you to class on time."

"Creep," Jody muttered, turning her attention to Mr. Miles, who was handing out mimeographed charts.

Mr. Miles looked up as Laura sauntered into the class. "I hope you have a good reason for being late, Miss Fielding."

For a moment Laura looked flustered, but she regained her composure almost at once. "Mrs. French just posted the cast list," she explained coolly. "I had to double-check my choices."

"Not on my time," the teacher said. "You've got morning detention tomorrow."

Jody couldn't even enjoy the fact that Laura was in trouble. All she could think about was that Laura had seen the list.

"There is no way I am going to be able to sit through a whole hour of 'deviant behaviors,' " she whispered to Marlie. "I've got to see that list!"

"There's no way Miles will let you out of class," Marlie retorted.

"I'll faint if I have to, I've got to see that list."

"Your attention, please," Mr. Miles's stern voice quieted the class. "Today we're going to be learning about paranoids." Marlie started to giggle. But to Jody his voice became garbled as she watched the second hand slowly tick off the minutes. She was desperate to see who was cast. Forty-five minutes seemed much too long to wait, but Mr. Miles was notorious for never letting anyone out of class early.

Going to the bathroom was out of the question, Jody thought. Too many had tried that ploy before. Fainting was sounding better by the minute. Then, like the sun breaking through the clouds on a gloomy day, Jody had an idea. Hiccups, she thought. A loud case of hiccups could give her the opportunity she needed. She could be excused long enough to check the cast list and miraculously recover. Mr. Miles would think of the hiccups as a disruption and ask her to leave. *Well, here goes,* Jody thought. *I'll get to test my true acting abilities.*

"Hic." Jody subtly jumped. "Hic." She moved again, catching Marlie's attention who covered her face to keep from laughing. "Hic," Jody repeated, starting to cause a stir. "Hic." Other class members began to titter. "Hiccup." Jody increased the volume and raised her hand. She figured the timing was right to ask for her exit.

"What is it, Jody?" Mr. Miles asked, perturbed.

"I seem to—hic—have the hiccups. May I please be excused to get a drink of water?"

"Hold your breath," Mr. Miles answered abruptly, turning back to the blackboard.

"I don't believe him," Jody whispered to Marlie. "I think if I fainted he'd let me lie here and rot."

"There's only a half an hour until lunch. We'll check it then," Marlie murmured.

Jody sighed and slumped in her desk chair.

Mr. Miles droned on and on, and by the time

the bell finally rang Jody was sure she had aged fifty years. She tried to look casual as she all but raced to the door.

Laura got there first. "Don't bother rushing," she said to Jody. "Beth and Ann and Marlie are all in the chorus," she went on. "And that's all from this class."

Jody was numb. Her stomach churned, and her head felt light. She looked at Marlie, whose eyes were full of mixed emotions.

"Congratulations," Jody said sincerely, giving Marlie a hug.

"It isn't fair," Marlie answered. "You're a better dancer than I am. You should have at least made the chorus. Oh, Jody, you should be doing the lead."

"But I'm not," Jody said, trying to smile.

"There must be a mistake. Let's go check the list ourselves."

"Not now, maybe later," Jody mumbled. "I need time to think."

"We'll talk about it during lunch," Marlie promised. "Maybe food will make you feel better."

"*Nothing* will make me feel better, especially not cafeteria food," Jody said as they entered the traffic in the hall. "I'll meet you later, Marlie. I just need some time to be alone."

"Are you sure?" Marlie asked sympathetically. "Remember, no matter what, I'm still your best friend."

"Always," Jody answered, and the girls hugged each other.

Marlie walked away slowly, looking over her shoulder.

As the reality of the news set in, Jody felt sure she was going to cry. The crowds in the hall made her feel as if she were a sardine being packed in a can. She knew she had to get out, away from the sounds of the students, the humiliation. She turned around and found the closest door that led out of the school.

As she stepped into the crisp Colorado air, Jody's tears began to flow. She walked out across the snow-covered lawn toward a small evergreen tree. *I hoped for too much*, she thought. *Why did I ever think I'd be cast? My plan was stupid.* By the time she sank down against the base of the tree, Jody was sobbing. It didn't matter that she was getting colder and wetter by the minute; she couldn't face going back into the school. All she wanted was to have a good cry.

Gradually, Jody realized that she had to look at the list posted in Mrs. French's room, if only to satisfy her own curiosity. She had to know whether Jeff had been cast, and she was curious about Tom. The thought of him sent a rush of warmth through her.

Jody's mind slipped back to their audition.

48

When they'd read together, Tom had made her feel relaxed and confident. He'd joked with her and encouraged her until she'd forgotten her fears and was aware only of his steel blue eyes and their nearly hypnotic effect. She wasn't even sure it had been real. No one had ever had quite that effect on her before. Jody sighed. She wanted to see Tom again almost as much as she wanted to be in the play.

But that's all behind me, Jody told herself as the sobbing finally stopped. *I won't cry anymore. I'm going to march up to the list and just look at it, no tears, no nothing. Then I'll find Marlie, and we'll set a time to celebrate.*

With the determination of a soldier heading into battle, Jody marched back into the school. She brushed her hair out of her eyes, blew her nose, squared her shoulders, held her head high, and entered Mrs. French's room.

The classroom looked empty. She cautiously glanced toward Mrs. French's desk and saw her eating a sandwich.

"I'm sorry to interrupt your lunch," Jody began.

Mrs. French smiled. "That's why I'm here. The list just went up, and I wanted the students to be able to check it during their lunch hour."

"I'd kind of forgotten all about it," Jody said

trying to sound casual. "But I have some old friends from Bradford who tried out."

"I see," Mrs. French said.

Jody smiled courageously as she scanned the list. She started with the chorus. She saw Marlie's name, Beth's, Ann's, and a girl she'd known in junior high who was going to Bradford. Her disappointment grew as she saw that Tom Arnold was playing the sheriff. He was doing the show, and she'd never see him again. Then Jody's saw Jeff's name, he was playing Og, the leprechaun. She wasn't sure she could keep up this facade much longer, and fresh tears welled up in her eyes. Half of her plan had worked out, the *wrong* half. With her heart in her throat, Jody looked to see who was playing *her* part. Who would be the girl to kiss Jeff Reynolds? She closed her eyes for an instant, then ran her finger down the rest of the list of lead characters until she found Susan the Silent. Slowly she followed the line across to reveal the lucky girl's name: Jordan—

"That's me!" Jody shouted. "I'm in the play. That's me, Jordan Bauer!"

"Not only are you in the play, you're the lead dancer," Mrs. French said with amusement.

"I am, really I am?" Jody said, astonished.

"You had a wonderful audition and deserve the part."

"But Laura said—" Jody moaned, double-checking her own name on the list.

"Laura doesn't always say the right things."

"Maybe she didn't realize that's my name. Jody is short for Jordan."

"Well, congratulations on getting the role," Mrs. French said.

"I promise to work very, very hard. I won't let you down," Jody blurted out as she headed for the door.

"Wait a minute," said the teacher, laughing. "You have to initial your name on the list to make it official."

"And I hope you'll be able to attend the cast get-acquainted party," she said as Jody took a red pencil from her purse and boldly engraved J.B. by her name. "It's on Saturday night at six, at my house."

"I'll be there," Jody said, practically jumping out of her skin.

"Have your mother call me if she has any questions."

"Thanks again," Jody said, vigorously shaking Mrs. French's hand. "This is the best day of my life!"

Chapter Five

"This party is the most exciting thing that's happened to me in a long time," Marlie said quietly, taking off her coat and hanging it in Mrs. French's closet.

"Ditto," Jody answered, following suit. "Do you know how long it's been since I've been to a party that wasn't either a family gathering or all girls?"

"Oh, so that explains why you changed your clothes a jillion times."

"I had to be sure I wore the right thing." She was thinking of Tom, hoping that he'd be there, too.

"For you or for Jeff?" Marlie asked, tousling Jody's hair.

"Quit that," Jody replied, walking to the mirror. "I chose this outfit because I liked it the best."

"You look great, too," Marlie said, touching up her makeup.

"Except for the braces," Jody grumbled, putting on lipstick. "You know there are only six kids in our class who still wear braces, and five of them are nerds."

"Yeah, who's the cool one?"

"Very funny," Jody said, pushing Marlie into the hallway. "Let's join the party."

They walked down the hall into the Frenchs' large family room. A roaring fire was blazing, and the furniture had been pushed back so that several tables could be set up. The spacious wooden cathedral ceiling echoed with the sounds of Irish music and high school students' laughter.

"Hi, Marlie, Jody," Laura said, posing in her bright red jumpsuit and matching high heels. "I hope you're ready for a lot of hard work. My choreography is very intricate, you know."

"I think I'm prepared," Jody said. She wondered if Laura was going to be this difficult through the two months of rehearsal.

"You know, Jordan, this show is going to be a lot harder than a ballet recital."

"If you knew her name was Jordan, why didn't you announce that she got the part in psychology class?" Marlie demanded.

"I must have forgotten, or maybe I thought Jordan was someone from Bradford."

"Jordan's my legal name," Jody explained. "My folks named me after a character in *The Great Gatsby*."

Laura looked bored. "Sorry, but it all worked out, anyway, right?" Without waiting for an answer, she turned and walked away.

"She is so mean," Jody muttered through clenched teeth.

"And spoiled," Marlie added. "But you've got to admit she's awfully pretty."

"Who's pretty?" Jeff asked, sneaking up behind them.

"Mrs. French's house," Marlie said quickly.

"Yes, don't you think this is a pretty room?" Jody added.

"Not as pretty as you two," he said with a grin.

The girls giggled, and Jody unconsciously covered her mouth.

"Either of you seen Laura?"

"No," Marlie lied. "Maybe she's working on her choreography tonight."

"Oh, I doubt it," Jeff said. "Laura's a party girl. We even met at a party—this same get-acquainted shindig for last year's play." He winked at Jody. "I always fall for my leading lady."

"Really," Jody answered with a catch in her throat.

"Is Laura planning to make the dances hard?" Marlie asked, changing the subject and elbowing Jody in the ribs.

Jeff shrugged. "She said something about changing Susan's stuff."

Jody could have killed Marlie for what she said next. "For a party girl, Laura hasn't been too friendly, especially to Jody. Is she always like that?"

"Oh, she likes to control everything." Jeff looked amused. "In each class she zeros in on some girl who might threaten her popularity. And then I told her I voted at the cheerleader elections for Jody instead of her friend Beth. Well, I guess Jody became next on her list."

"But Beth won," Jody said, running her hand through her hair in disbelief.

"That doesn't matter. She's weird about things like that. Look, there's Laura now. See you later."

"Well, at least I know the reason," Jody remarked after Jeff was out of sight.

"Yeah, but since you're playing opposite Jeff in the show, she's going to make it really tough on you."

"May I have your attention, please," Mrs. French called, after turning down the music.

"Welcome to the cast get-acquainted party. There are name cards at each table, so after you go through the buffet line, please sit in your assigned seats."

Jody and Marlie followed the others toward the food. Everywhere they looked there was something Irish. A large rainbow covered the wall behind the buffet. There were shamrocks, shillelaghs, and leprechauns on the tables, and green balloons and streamers hung from the corners of the room. And, of course, the dinner was completely Irish—corned beef and cabbage, soda bread, a special spiced grog, boiled potatoes, and Irish pork cake for dessert.

"There are all these people here I've never seen before," Jody said, trying to balance her dinner plate.

Marlie took a slice of cake and stepped out of line. "I think the orchestra and stage crew members are here, too."

"This is so exciting. Now if I can just make it to my seat without dropping this food."

"Perhaps we should have checked where we were sitting first," Marlie said, trying to maintain her own balancing act.

"Over here," Jeff called, motioning the girls to his table. "You're both sitting over here."

"What luck," Jody said, maneuvering to the table and setting down her plate and drink.

"Here, let me help," said a familiar voice.

"Oh, it's you," Jody said, spinning around on her heels.

"You can call me Tom," he teased, pulling out Jody's chair so she could sit down.

"Thanks," she said, sitting down. "You sure did help me during the auditions. You were great."

"You didn't need my help," Tom said. "I knew you'd be cast as soon as I saw you dancing in the hall."

"That was you?"

Tom shrugged. "I was on my way to my locker."

"I felt so stupid."

"You were just practicing, and it looks like it paid off, too."

"Thanks," Jody answered, raising her grog.

"To *Finian's Rainbow*," Tom added as the others at the table joined in the toast.

"Cheers," Marlie said, clinking the glass of the boy from Bradford named Doug who was sitting next to her. "What are you doing in the show?"

Doug bowed and answered, "Meet the orchestra's one and only drummer."

Jody watched with amusement as Marlie and Doug instantly launched into an enthusiastic conversation. She turned to Tom curiously.

"Have you ever done a show before?" she asked, trying to avoid staring into his eyes.

"Well," he answered with a grin, "if you count the turnip in my fourth-grade play, then I guess I have. What about you?"

"I've only been in dance recitals," Jody admitted. "I'm a terrible singer. You're playing the sheriff, aren't you?"

"Yeah, it's a fairly small part, but I do get some solo lines to sing."

The thought of it made Jody wince. "I could never sing in front of a group of people."

"Well, I could never dance, so I guess Mrs. French cast us in the right roles. I always envied Fred Astaire in those old movies. He sure could move."

"He's one of my favorites, too. I loved him with Ginger Rogers, but my favorite was when he danced with Cyd Charisse in *The Band Wagon.*"

"Yeah, but nothing beats *Holiday Inn* with all that snow."

"You like snow, too?" Jody asked. "Everybody gives me such a hard time because winter is my favorite season." Jody leaned her elbows on the table. She was under his spell again.

"They think I'm crazy because I'd rather go skiing than lie on the beach," Tom said, rolling his eyes in despair.

"Me, too," Jody said with surprise. "I'm afraid to ask you what your favorite food is—so if you say spaghetti, I'm going into shock."

"You missed that one." He leaned in so close their foreheads practically touched. "My favorite food is lasagna."

"You've got weird taste in food," Jody said with a giggle.

"Hey, what's going on over here? Did you miss me?" Jeff demanded as he sat down next to Jody. "I had to calm Laura down. She's upset because she's seated with the technical crew, and she thinks they're all jerks."

"Justice lives," Marlie whispered to Jody, lifting her soda bread.

As if on cue, Laura immediately rushed over to their table. "I can't stand it over there any longer," she complained, sitting on the arm of Jeff's chair. "Mrs. French made a mistake, or someone must have switched the name cards. Those must be your friends, Jody. Why don't you sit with them?"

"No thank you, Laura," Jody said with exaggerated sweetness. "I'm comfortable right here."

"But they *are* your friends," Laura insisted.

"Well, maybe if you'd talk to them for a while they'd be your friends, too," Jody stated.

"Get serious."

Tom shot Laura a look of disbelief, and for

the first time Laura noticed him. "You play the sheriff, don't you?"

Tom nodded.

"You were really good in auditions." Then despite the fact that Jeff's arm was on her waist, Laura began to sweet-talk Tom.

"I think I'm going to be sick," Jody said under her breath.

"Ignore it," Marlie whispered back. "It doesn't mean anything. She just shifts into 'automatic flirt' whenever she's near a good-looking guy."

"May I have your attention again?" Mrs. French broke in, clinking her spoon against her glass. "When everyone is finished with dinner, please return to your original chairs. We're going to play a game that will allow you to practice your acting abilities."

"Terrific," Jody muttered. The evening had been going downhill ever since Laura appeared at their table. But at least Mrs. French's announcement meant that Laura would be leaving them soon.

"Attention please," Mrs. French called a few minutes later. "Underneath each chair is a piece of green construction paper with a word written on it. Have the person sitting to your left pin the word on your back with the safety pin provided in the corner. But don't you look at it. Then one at a time, show the rest of the people at your table your word. They must give you nonverbal clues so you can guess what the word is. You can test your acting abilities by seeing how well you can mime the clues. Remember, no talking."

"Here," Tom said, taking the card from Jody. Gently, he moved her hair to the side and pinned the word on her back. "You should be good at this," he predicted. "Susan the Silent's role is all 'nonverbal clues.' " He turned Jody around to face him. "There you go, all set." For a moment they just stood there and smiled at each other.

Jody felt herself blushing. If Tom was any good at reading 'nonverbal clues,' he'd know exactly how she felt. She wondered if her heart would ever slow down again.

Jeff broke her reverie. "Give me a hand here, Jod," he said. "You wouldn't make me pin this card on all by myself, would you?"

"Guess not," she replied absently. Even as she worked on Jeff's card her eyes kept wandering to Tom. No one had ever made her feel like this.

"Who wants to go first?" Doug asked.

"Not me," Marlie and Jody answered together.

"I'll go," Tom offered and turned to reveal the word *shamrock* on his card. "Okay," he said, turning back and looking directly at Jody. "I'm ready for those clues."

Marlie went first, holding up four fingers, but Tom guessed "fortune." When Doug acted out a man buying a lottery ticket and winning, Tom guessed "sweepstakes."

Finally it was Jody's turn. She carefully pretended to be walking through a field. She picked a few flowers and smelled them. Then she stepped back in mock surprise, pointed to something on the ground, and picked it up. Slowly, she mimed pulling off four leaves and then jumping up and down happily.

"Shamrock," Tom guessed, giving her a smile that made her feel as if something had lit up inside her.

Marlie went next, easily guessing the color green. Doug had a little difficulty with "potato," and Jeff finally gave up and cheated by looking at his "pot of gold."

Jody was the only one left, and suddenly she realized she was nervous. She'd been good at giving clues to others, but would she be as good at figuring out her own word? She glanced in Tom's direction, and he gave her an encouraging smile that immediately made her feel better. No doubt about it—she was falling for him, and fast.

Jody turned around to show her word to the others. At once everyone started laughing. Marlie looked funny when she gave her clue—rock or stone, Jody thought. Doug wasn't any better; he acted like a limbo dancer. Tom thrilled her by taking her hand and kissing it, and then Jeff really threw her for a loop. He firmly grabbed Jody by the shoulders and then slowly started to bend down to kiss her. Jody's mind whirled, and her knees felt like wet noodles. Then, just before he reached her lips, Jeff moved his head and kissed her on the forehead.

Jody was stunned. Everyone was waiting for her answer, but her heart was beating too fast for her to speak. Quickly she tried to regain her composure by reviewing the clues. *Rock, limbo, kiss, kiss. What can it be?* she wondered. She was determined not to give up, and she wasn't going to cheat like Jeff. Suddenly it hit her. "The Blarney Stone," she shouted.

"Right," Marlie answered.

Jeff came up behind her and unpinned the card from her back. "I would have really kissed you"—he started to grin—"but I didn't want to risk permanent damage from your braces."

"That's okay," Jody said, closing her mouth over her teeth.

"But don't worry about it in the show," Jeff said. "I know how to kiss you on the side of the mouth so that the audience will think it's real."

"Swell," Jody said, trying to hide her embarrassment. "I think I'll help Mrs. French and get rid of these paper plates." Relieved to get away from Jeff, she headed for the kitchen.

"Hey, slow down." Jody turned to see Tom behind her, balancing two enormous salad bowls. "You were sharp in that game," he said. "You're going to make a terrific Susan the Silent."

Jody pushed open the kitchen door. "I don't think Jeff Reynolds thinks so."

Tom set his bowls down and then helped her get rid of the paper plates. "Look," he said gently, "don't let Jeff get you down. I don't really know him, but from what I can see he just says or does whatever amuses him."

"My ten-year-old brother has more tact!" Jody said angrily.

Tom gave her a long, careful look. "I think," he said, "that when you're on stage with Og, every guy in the audience is going to wish he were Jeff. And I think Jeff knows it."

"Thank you," Jody said. "Thanks a lot. Maybe we'll have some scenes together," she added shyly.

"I hope so," he said. "That would be fun."

Mrs. French's voice carried into the kitchen, "Rehearsals begin on Monday evening at seven P.M. at Edgeworth. If you haven't gotten a script yet, check one out from me before you leave tonight."

"I'd better get a script," Tom said, "and find whether we really are onstage together. I guess I'll see you Monday night." He winked at her. "It was nice having dinner with you, even if I did have to switch the place cards to do it."

"You changed the cards?" Jody asked in amazement.

"How else could I be sure I'd sit with you?"

Jody laughed. "Don't let Laura find out."

"See you Monday," Tom said.

"Right." Jody watched him cross the room, excited by the prospect of seeing him again so soon. She knew it was only a rehearsal, but Tom sounded as if he really wanted to see her.

Since Jody already had her script, she went to get her coat and purse and find Marlie. But when she picked up her things she noticed Marlie's were already gone. *Where did she go?* Jody wondered. *She wouldn't have left without me.* Finally she found Marlie standing beside the front door with Doug. Marlie was handing him a piece of paper. Jody watched, puzzled, but a few moments later, after Doug had left, Marlie cleared up the mystery. "He asked me for my phone number," she said excitedly. "These guys from Bradford are different."

"Yeah," Jody agreed as they walked out to Marlie's car.

"Did you see his gorgeous gray-green eyes?" Marlie asked.

"No, they're blue. Definitely blue."

"They're green," Marlie insisted. "Oh, you must mean Jeff's, but I thought they were brown."

"They are," Jody answered absently.

"Then whose eyes are blue?"

"Tom's," Jody said with a smile.

Chapter Six

"Which one looks better for rehearsal?" Jody asked Marlie. She held up a blue cotton jumpsuit next to an oversize sweatshirt, and black stretch pants.

"Either one," Marlie said, throwing up her arms in exasperation, "or any of the six you tried on before that. You looked great in the first outfit, two hours ago."

"Which one was that?" Jody dug through a pile of skirts, sweaters, and shoes.

"It looks like a hurricane hit this place," Marlie said, laughing as she plopped down on Jody's twin bed.

Jody glared at her friend. "Some help you are. The most important day of my life, and you're making jokes."

"All right," Marlie said, sitting up straight. "It

should be something you can dance in and that won't show sweat."

"And that Tom might like."

"You mean Jeff, don't you?" Marlie said, sounding surprised.

"Umm—I might as well look good for both of them," Jody said nervously. For some reason, she wasn't quite ready to admit that she had a crush on Tom.

"Whatever. Just hurry; we have only twenty minutes until rehearsal starts." Marlie picked up her purse and headed down the Bauer staircase.

Jody trailed Marlie out to Marlie's car. "I'm glad at least one of us is old enough to drive. It sure is nice of your dad to let you take the car to rehearsal every night," Jody said. She gave Marlie a curious look as Marlie backed out of the driveway. "Is Doug going to be there tonight?" Jody asked.

"He said they'll be practicing in the band room," Marlie replied. "But, changing the subject, I think Tom's cute. And I think he likes you."

As they drew close to the school, Jody debated how much she should tell Marlie. At last she said, "All I know is I never would have gotten through that audition without him. And he was easy to talk to at the party, too. You know something, Marl, I just realized my heart beats fast when Tom's around, but I don't get all flustered and weird like when I talk to Jeff."

"Sounds like love to me," Marlie said, pulling into a parking spot.

"Are you sure?" Jody asked as she got out of the car. "I don't even have words for it. But every time I look at Tom, it's like a jolt goes right through me. Maybe you're right. After all, you've already had boyfriends."

"Boyfriend," Marlie corrected, "and that wasn't love. It was a mistake. You've got to be careful. Sometimes when you think it's Mr. Right, it's really Mr. Wrong."

Like Jeff, Jody added silently.

The girls joined the cast in the auditorium where Mrs. French explained the evening's rehearsal schedule. Jody tried to pay attention, but she couldn't help looking for Tom. Finally, she saw him sitting next to Doug in the back of the auditorium. He looked so handsome, Jody thought, with his straight dark hair catching the lights from the stage.

"There are the guys," Jody whispered to Marlie. "Maybe we'll get to talk to them before we start."

"So if there are no questions," Mrs. French said, finishing, "let's start rehearsal. Laura, you take the dancers to the cafeteria."

Jody and Marlie were both in Laura's group. They hesitated for a moment as Marlie caught the boys' attention. Doug waved, and then Tom met them at the auditorium door.

Tom held up his script and moaned in mock despair. "I've already forgotten all my lines."

"I'm nervous, too," Jody admitted.

"You?" he said. "You don't even have any lines to forget!"

"Just an entire dance solo," Jody said as indignantly as she could.

"And here comes the choreographer," Marlie muttered as Laura strode toward them.

"Jody and Marlie, you're supposed to be in the cafeteria," Laura snapped without even pausing to look at them.

"She's sweet tempered," Tom observed.

"You noticed." Jody gave him a wry grin. "I guess we'd better go."

"Don't worry about Laura," Tom said. "You'll do just fine."

Although Tom's words made Jody feel better, they weren't exactly accurate. "This is rehearsal time, Jody, and you're late," were the first words Laura said as Jody and Marlie entered the cafeteria. Before Jody could point out that most of the dancers hadn't even shown up yet, Laura flipped on a tape recorder and quickly executed eight counts of a routine. Jody couldn't help being impressed. Laura's form was graceful and precise, and the combinations she put together were absolutely beautiful. She might be obnoxious, Jody realized, but she deserved to be the choreographer.

Laura finished the combination with a dramatic leap. "Now you do it, Jody," she said, not even out of breath.

"I—I'm not sure how to start," Jody stammered. "Could you do it again, slowly first?"

Laura shook her head impatiently. "You're going to have to pay close attention if you're ever going to get through the show."

"I'll try," Jody said, embarrassed.

"You step to the right, hop left, hop right, pivot right, arabesque, turn to the right, pose, and leap.

"Sloppy," was all Laura said when Jody finished.

Jody breathed an audible sigh of relief as Laura critically surveyed the rest of the group and had everyone do the routine together.

"The next combination starts, balance, balance, scissor kick, pirouette turns one, two, three," Laura explained as the group stumbled along with her. "Now you do it, Jody, and try to concentrate this time."

"All right," Jody said with determination. "Balance, balance, scissor kick—"

"Wrong, wrong, wrong," Laura snapped. "Scissor kick is on the left."

"I'm sorry," Jody said, falling over her own feet. "Let me try again."

Jody took a deep breath and started from the beginning. Carefully, she counted each step as she moved through the combination.

"That was better," Laura said quietly. "So if you're ready we'll go on to the next eight counts."

"Great." Jody sighed, looking over her shoulder at Marlie for encouragement.

"Hang in there," Marlie whispered, giving Jody the thumbs-up sign.

Laura continued to push Jody, but Jody made herself keep up even when the others had difficulty, and to her surprise she found she was enjoying herself.

"Not bad," Laura was forced to say after they finished blocking the first number. She gave Jody a reluctant smile, then called for a ten-minute break.

"You're doing great, Jody," Marlie said as the girls limped toward the water fountain.

"I think Laura is dying to replace me."

"Well, no one else can do the steps, either, so she'll have to replace all of us."

Jody noticed the other kids coming out of the auditorium. "Look, the actors are taking a break, too. Do you see the guys anywhere?"

"No, but if we sit by the auditorium entrance, they're bound to see us."

"Now you're thinking," Jody said. A table and folding chairs had been set up in the hallway outside the auditorium, and the two girls sat down. A moment later Doug came out of the band room looking as exhausted as Jody felt.

"Where do I find the soda machine?" he asked. "I'm dying of thirst."

At once Marlie jumped up and offered to give him a guided tour of Edgeworth.

Alone at last, Jody thought, stretching her legs across Marlie's chair and lying down.

"Quick, medic!" Tom's voice pierced her solitude. "Dying dancer, dying dancer!" He sat down on the floor beside her. "How's it going?"

"It's hard work," Jody admitted, pleased that he'd sought her out. "Every muscle in my body is going to hurt tomorrow." She turned her head toward him; it was weird trying to conduct a conversation horizontally. Jody started to sit up.

"No, don't get up," Tom ordered in a very official-sounding voice. "Dr. Arnold will work his magic on your feet."

"I'm ticklish," Jody said, starting to pull away.

"I'm not going to tickle your feet. I'm going to massage them." Tom sat down beside her, gently lifted her tattered ballet slippers, and placed them in his lap. Although Jody was mortified to have anyone really look at her ragged shoes, the thought of a foot massage was too enticing to resist.

"So what's it like being the sheriff?" Jody asked. "Any resemblance to being a turnip in the vegetable play?"

"Close," Tom said with a smile.

"Maybe I should have tried out for the basket-weaving club or the volleyball team or even soccer," Jody said. "Any one of them would have been easier."

"What? And give up show business?" Tom gave her left foot a final pat and stood up, holding his hand out to her.

"Time's up," Mrs. French called. "Everyone into the auditorium, and let's put it together."

"Great," said Tom, "now I'll get to see you dance."

"What?" Jody cried, panic-stricken. "I can't do this in front of anyone!"

Tom grinned. "And what were you planning to do when there's an audience?"

"I'll do it *then*. Not *now*. I'm not ready."

Tom looked as if he was trying hard to keep a straight face. "Now this is just a hunch," he said, "but it may be easier to do it *then* if you do it *now*. Come on," he continued more gently, "it's just a rehearsal."

What am I going to do? Jody thought, as panic froze every muscle. She gave Tom a desperate look and reluctantly went into the auditorium.

"If I can remember the first and last combinations, I'll be all right," she mumbled to herself as the others ambled in.

"Cast onstage," Mrs. French called. "We'll do the scene we blocked and then go right into the dance."

Jody barely heard the lines of dialogue as she stared at the floor, mentally going through each step. Tom's voice caught her attention, and she looked up to watch him do his blocking and dialogue. *He looks so relaxed*, Jody thought, wondering if anyone could see her knees shake. Then before she knew it, the music started and she was dancing.

It seemed as if the moment she began to move every eye zeroed in on her. For a moment Jody froze, and then her eyes found Tom smiling at her. Jody began to dance again, the panic gone. The first difficult combination was done, then the second, third, fourth, and even the fifth and final movements flowed. A few floppy arms and some off-balance turns, but at least she'd gotten through it.

"A good start," Mrs. French said as the cast gathered together.

Jeff shook her hand with a little too much enthusiasm. "You were terrific!" he exclaimed.

"Not bad," said Tom with a grin.

"What about my choreography?" Laura said, linking her arm through Jeff's. "Don't I get any credit?"

"Sure you do, Laura," Jeff replied. "But you'll never sparkle onstage like Jody does."

"What?" Jody said. That sounded corny, even for Jeff.

"Sure," Jeff continued, looking straight at her and obviously trying not to laugh. "I was out in the audience, and with the stage lights bouncing off those braces, you sparkled to the last row."

Jody looked at Jeff in disbelief. Everything that had once seemed "magic" about him was suddenly, irretrievably gone.

"Shut up, Reynolds," Marlie snapped. "Lots of kids wear braces and—"

Jody never heard the rest of it. Mortified, she turned and ran backstage.

In the small space behind the curtain, Jody slumped against the wall and slid wearily to the floor. *Jeff and Laura are a good pair*, she thought angrily. *Neither of them cares what they say or do as long as it makes them the center of attention.* It was bad enough being self-conscious about her braces without Jeff

Reynolds making it worse. Jody tried to summon up the courage to continue the rehearsal, but the thought of her scene with Jeff made her sick. *How am I going to feel comfortable smiling around him, let alone kissing him?* she wondered. *Well, I don't want him to be my first kiss,* she decided as she stood up and straightened her sweater. But even with that matter resolved, Jody found it difficult to go back to the rehearsal. Instead she settled for counting the nicks in the wooden floorboards.

"Hey," said a gentle voice. "You okay back there?" Tom carefully peered around the side curtain.

"Yeah, sure," Jody answered, still staring at the floor.

Tom leaned against the wall and studied her. "You're not going to let that egomaniac get to you, are you?"

Jody shrugged.

"He probably didn't even realize what he was saying."

"That doesn't excuse it!" Jody said angrily.

"No, it doesn't." Tom followed her eyes. "That's a fascinating floor we've got here."

Jody ignored him; she wasn't ready to be cheered up yet.

"But despite the charms of the floor," he went

on, "you're going to have to look up for a minute and give me an answer."

Jody lifted her head and glared at him.

"Am I going to have to tickle you to get you to smile again?" Tom backed Jody up against the stage wall. He was so close, she could feel his breath brush against her cheek. "I'm not letting you go back to rehearsal until I get a smile."

Jody grinned in spite of herself. "All right," she gave in, "I guess I'd better get back to work." Slowly, she slid past Tom and made her way back to the cafeteria.

The next two hours of rehearsal went quickly. With her determination in tact, Jody ignored Laura's sarcastic remarks and concentrated on the combinations. Even when Laura paired her with Jeff and began showing them their duet, Jody managed to remain cool and professional.

Surprisingly, her act fooled everyone but Jeff. "What's the matter?" he asked.

"Nothing." Jody's voice was flat and distant.

"You're not sore because I teased you about your braces, are you?"

"Not anymore," Jody answered frankly. "But I didn't exactly enjoy it."

"Hey, look, I'm sorry," Jeff said, taking her hand. "But they really did sparkle."

Jody stared at him blankly, feeling nothing. She was actually relieved when Laura stepped between them, asking if they wouldn't mind concentrating on the steps.

They finished the second number just moments before Mrs. French called the cast together for a note session. This was the part of rehearsal in which she gave them all feedback on their work. Jody waited for her own critique, mentally replaying every mistake she'd made.

Finally, Mrs. French called her name, and gave her a sympathetic look. "There's one very important thing you need to do, my dear."

"What?" Jody asked in a small voice.

Mrs. French smiled. "Relax."

By the time notes were over, Jody was exhausted. She gathered her things and started to walk to the parking lot. It had been a strange first rehearsal. Laura had made her feel terrible, Tom had made her feel wonderful, and Jeff had made her want to crawl under the stage. As much as she hated him for embarrassing her, she was glad of one thing—she had finally seen him for what he was.

"Hi." Jody looked up to see Tom leaning against the exit door.

"Hi," she answered, smiling carefully so her braces wouldn't show.

"Feeling better?" he asked gently.

"Thanks to Dr. Arnold," Jody said. "The backstage talk helped, and I never did get a chance to thank you for the foot massage."

"I'll send you my bill on opening night," Tom promised as they walked out of the building together. "You know," he said, "you really were good. Are you sure you haven't performed before?"

"Positive." Jody felt herself blush and quickly changed the subject. "You haven't seen Marlie, have you? She's driving me home."

"Nope, but I'll bet she's with Doug and he's driving *me* home." Tom gave a very theatrical bow in the direction of the parking lot. "May I escort you to the car?"

"I'd be honored, sir," Jody answered with a giggle.

They walked for a few minutes without speaking. Jody felt as if she were suddenly more aware of everything around her—Tom walking beside her, the stars in the evening sky, the sound of their feet on the blacktop, even the cold wind against her cheeks.

"It's really cold out here," she said with a shiver. "I must not have cooled down completely."

"Here, see if this helps." Tom took off his long black-and-orange scarf and wrapped it around Jody's shoulders.

He stood close, and Jody's knees were shaky

again. The scarf felt warm, and it smelled like a mixture of Tom and his spicy cologne.

"Much better, thanks," she said.

"Isn't that Marlie over there?" Tom asked, sounding somehow sorry that he'd spotted them.

"With Doug," Jody finished.

Tom grinned as they approached the car. "It looks like we're going to interrupt something important."

"Maybe we should make some noise or something," Jody suggested.

"I'm not sure even an earthquake would stop a kiss like that."

Jody cleared her throat loudly.

"Beautiful night, don't you think?" Tom practically shouted as they neared Marlie's car.

Marlie and Doug quickly stepped away from each other, Doug turning on Tom with an irritated look.

Tom shrugged apologetically. "Sorry to break things up, but I have a geometry test to study for tomorrow."

"Me, too," Doug admitted with a smile. He turned to Marlie and said a very soft good night.

Jody only had eyes for Tom. "See you at rehearsal tomorrow night," she said.

They stood for a minute like statues on the lawn. It was Jody who started things moving by opening Marlie's car door and jumping in. The silence was broken, and the guys were gone.

"I can't believe that kiss," Jody said as Marlie started the car.

"What kiss?" Marlie asked coyly.

"I knew it," Jody said. "You really like him, don't you?"

Marlie laughed softly. "He's pretty special."

"Tell me about the kiss. What did he say?"

"He didn't *say* anything." Marlie pulled out of the parking lot and looked very absorbed in the traffic.

"Did he ask you if he could kiss you?"

"Of course not, silly. He just kissed me."

"Was it nice?"

"What do you think?"

Jody knew she was asking dumb questions, but she couldn't help it; she had to know. "How did you keep from bumping noses?"

Marlie gave an exasperated moan. "He just leaned toward me, bent his head to the right, and I went to the left. That's how you avoid the noses. Actually, it's very romantic."

"I guess," Jody said with a sigh as they turned into their neighborhood.

"Once you start, it all happens naturally." Marlie assured her. "As long as you don't pucker up, you'll be fine."

By the time Marlie dropped Jody at her house,

Jody was trying to picture herself kissing Tom. She gave up; it was impossible to imagine herself really kissing anyone.

"Hey, kiddo," Bud called as she entered the house. "How's *Finian's Rainwear*?"

"*Rainbow*," Jody muttered, "and you know it."

"All right, all right," her brother said good-naturedly. "But tell me, what *is* that thing you're wearing around your shoulders? It's kind of a weird costume, if you ask me."

Jody looked down at herself and gasped in surprise. She was still wearing Tom's scarf. "Oh," was all she could say.

Bud grinned down at her. "Could be the next hot fashion at Edgeworth—"

"Oh, shut up." Jody couldn't help smiling as she took it off. She hung up her coat in the closet, and then when she was sure Bud wasn't watching, she carefully folded the scarf and brought it up to her room.

Jody took off her rehearsal clothes, pulled on a Denver Broncos nightshirt, and wrapped the scarf around her face and shoulders. *It smells and feels like he's standing right next to me*, she thought. With the music from the show playing in her head, she began a dreamy, swirling waltz. Finally she spun onto her bed and slipped under the cover.

"Max," she said, hugging her favorite teddy bear, "meet Tom's scarf." She carefully unwound the treasure and wrapped it around the bear. She turned out her night-light and slowly lay back on the pillow; then she closed her eyes to reenact her dream, leaned Max to the right, and she went to the left. Remembering Marlie's instructions, she kissed the bear. Somehow her braces had stuck to the bear's fur.

"I don't believe this," Jody mumbled, crawling out of bed in the dark. With one hand on the bear she fumbled through her desk drawer for a pair of scissors. After minor surgery and a close shave for Max, she slid back into bed.

"What a day," she said, holding the scarf-clad bear to her heart.

Chapter Seven

Jody couldn't believe how fast the weeks were going. School went by in a blur. Her days revolved around the show. She had practiced and practiced her dance solos until even Laura seemed satisfied. Each day brought her closer to the character of Susan the Silent. But it was the rehearsal breaks and the ten-minute talks with Tom that Jody lived for. She daydreamed about him constantly, and when he'd given her a valentine for Valentine's Day she finally let herself believe that braces or no, he really liked her as much as she liked him. The problem was that they were never really alone. There wasn't much chance for romance when they always seemed to be surrounded by at least half the cast.

On a clear, warm Saturday morning in the

first week of March, Jody rolled out of bed and went over to her window, amazed that most of the winter snow had already melted. She slipped into her blue jeans and a soft pink- purple- and blue-checked flannel shirt. Over that she put a royal-blue Shaker sweater vest and a thin purple belt. Since the ground was dry, she decided to wear her pink aerobic shoes. She had always loved the weekends, but in the seven weeks they'd been rehearsing, it meant two days each week without seeing Tom. *Funny how the play has changed so many things,* she thought, as she made her bed.

The rehearsal the day before had been extra special because Jody and Tom had worked on *their* scene in the show. It wasn't anything big, only a few minutes onstage, but it was so much fun. She was surprised at herself because for once she wasn't nervous. That might have been because just before they went onstage Tom had told her about his "surefire guaranteed-to-cure stage fright" remedy.

"What's that?" Jody asked skeptically.

"Just imagine everyone in the audience sitting there in their underwear."

Jody giggled at the image.

"See," he said. "It works. You're too busy laughing to be nervous."

During the break, Jody had playfully stolen

his cowboy hat. Tom retaliated by locking her in the stage jail and mischievously dangling the key just out of her reach. He was deciding what bail Jody was going to have to pay when Mrs. French called for rehearsal to start again. The scene had gone smoothly, and now Jody wished it were Friday all over again.

Jody wrinkled her nose and dabbed on a little blush and some mascara. She pulled her hair back into a ponytail and sprayed on some perfume. Now she was ready, she thought. For what, she didn't know, but she wanted to be prepared.

She was in the kitchen munching on a piece of toast when the phone rang.

"Glad I caught you," Marlie said.

"Why, what's up?" said Jody.

"Some of the cast is getting together for a picnic at Bittersweet Park."

"Is Tom going?" Jody asked, hoping she didn't sound as excited as she felt.

"I don't know. Doug hasn't gotten hold of him yet."

Jody sighed. "I promised my mom I'd clean out the garage on the first nice Saturday we had."

"Well, then come down to the park afterward. I'll keep Tom there if he comes," promised Marlie.

Jody was about to ask if Laura was going when the doorbell rang. When it rang for the second time, she realized that no one else in the family was going to answer it.

"Hey look, I've got to go," she told Marlie. "Someone's at the door. Call me back later, okay?" Jody set down her toast and headed for the front door. She didn't see a car out in the street, so she figured it wasn't one of her older brothers' friends.

"Who is it?" Jody asked as she opened the door.

"Hi, happy Saturday," Tom answered.

"Hi," Jody said, stunned. "What are you doing here? How'd you know where I live?"

"I have my vays of finding out," Tom said, using a mock-German accent as he leaned against the doorway. "I'm sorry I didn't call first, but I wasn't sure if I'd stop by."

"Getting up your nerve?" Jody teased.

"Something like that." Tom shrugged. "I thought you might like to go for a walk. I brought you a present, but you have to come outside to get it."

Jody giggled. "A present for me, really?"

"It's nothing big, but you have to come outside."

"Okay, let me get my vest, and write my mom a note, then I'll be right out." Jody closed the door and with a shiver of excitement put on her down vest, gloves, and tam. Then she wrote a quick note to her mom and hurried to the front yard, hoping this wasn't all a dream and that Tom would still be there.

Outside, Tom stood leaning against the knobby tires of his road bicycle, the winter sun dancing on his dark brown hair. Jody thought he looked adorable. He wore jeans and a blue-and-green plaid flannel shirt—the rugged look that Jody loved. His jean jacket was lying over his right shoulder, and he was holding something in his left hand behind his back. As Jody approached him, he held a kite out in front of him.

"For me?" Jody tilted her head shyly.

"Thought it looked like a great day for flying," Tom said as he licked his index finger and held it up to check the wind.

"I love kites," said Jody. "When I was a little girl, I used to get my mom one for her birthday every year, just so *I* could fly it." They both laughed. "I can't believe I told you that," Jody said, suddenly feeling a little self-conscious.

"Why not?" Tom winked at her. "It's a great idea. Besides, now I know what to get my mom for her birthday this year." Tom's dimples deepened when he laughed. *He's so neat*, Jody thought, tingling with excitement.

Behind the Bauer home was a huge cornfield.

Traces of corn stalks still remained, but Tom and Jody found an open flat spot to put the kite together. The kite was black-and-white plastic and shaped like a bat, with a long tail. Tom tied the string on it, and Jody found a slender branch to slide through the cardboard tube holding the twine.

"Ready for takeoff, copilot?" Tom called.

"Ten-four, pilot," Jody replied, using her left hand as a microphone.

Tom stood up and tossed some dried weeds into the air, rechecking the wind velocity. "Here goes nothing," he said, starting to run through the field with the kite. He darted among the corn stalks, around the weeds, and down the furrows.

Although the kite was going nowhere, Jody ran along, coaching Tom as they went. "Run left, now right," she called, circling around him. "Let out more string." Without realizing it, she was tangling them up like a spider in its web. The kite fluttered down and popped Tom on the head, and they both burst out laughing.

"Some copilot you are," Tom said with a chuckle. "I guess it would help if we had a breeze," he added, sitting down to untangle the string.

"Or a less clumsy copilot." Jody grinned. Sitting beside him, she unwound the string from around her ankle, tucked her knees under her chin, and tilted her head back in the sun. "I love days like today," she said with a sigh.

"Me, too. I wish every day were as perfect as today. You want to know a secret?" Tom said after a moment.

"Sure." She was glad he trusted her enough to tell her a secret.

Tom hesitated, tugged some more on the kite, and then plunged in. "I've always wanted to build a house with my own two hands, out in the open like this. I would have been a great pioneer." As he described the house, he drew the outline in the dirt with a stick. "A two-story A-frame, like this; four bedrooms, a den, entertainment room, and a great sun deck, here. And to top it off, a picket fence all around. Pretty corny, huh?"

"It sounds beautiful."

"Okay, now it's your turn," Tom urged.

"For what?"

"To tell a secret. You must have some secret or a dream you can tell."

"Well . . ." Jody rocked back and forth for a minute. "But I've never told anyone before. I guess that's what makes it a secret, huh?"

Tom nodded. "I won't tell anyone."

"All right," she started slowly, "I want to make an important contribution to life. A big drop in the bucket. I'm not sure what it is I want to do, but I have this fear of being ordinary or dull."

"You, dull?" Tom said with surprise. "Never."

Jody grinned. "That's not what my older brothers say— You want to know something else?"

"What?"

"I used to think Jeff Reynolds was great, but now that I know him better—I think I was crazy." Jody covered her head with her arms and buried her face in her knees.

Tom threw a blade of grass at her. "I think you were crazy, too." He stood up, taking the kite in one hand and holding the other out to Jody. "Good thing you came to your senses." He held her hand gently as they started to walk. The glow of the sun couldn't compare with the warm feeling Jody felt in her heart. She was definitely in love. They smiled at each other and walked through the field.

"Look," Tom said, "pussy willows."

"Aren't they pretty."

"For you then, miss." Tom picked the stems and did a low, princely bow.

Touched, Jody returned a curtsy and replied, "Why thank you, sir."

They walked along a grassy knoll, and under a large cottonwood tree, Jody found two cattails growing. Tom rounded out the collection with a milkweed stalk. "They're beautiful," Jody said, holding them out in front of her. She wouldn't have traded her bouquet for Miss America's roses. "I love them, and they'll last forever."

"I hope so." Tom gave Jody's hand a squeeze. They walked in silence until Jody heard the horn from Marlie's red car.

She looked up to see Marlie and Doug fiercely waving from the end of the Bauer driveway. "Hi," Jody shouted as she and Tom ran to find out what the emergency was.

"You guys going to the picnic or not?" Doug called out.

"Everybody got there over an hour ago," said Marlie. "We've just picked up the goodies." She pointed to a bucket of chicken and some sodas in a cooler in the backseat.

"So, hop in and let's get going," Doug added.

"You go ahead," Tom said to Jody.

"Don't you want to go?" Jody couldn't hide her disappointment.

"Sure, but you forgot I've got my own wheels."

"When did you get a car?" Doug asked, standing up.

"I didn't, it's my road bike."

"Oh, right, I forgot," Doug sat back down.

"So, you go ahead, Jod, and I'll ride down and meet you there—unless you want to ride with me."

"How?" Jody questioned hesitantly.

"On the handlebars, of course."

"Just remember you need your legs," Marlie said as she fastened her seat belt.

"And no side trips, Arnold," warned Doug.

"Send up flares if you need help," Marlie called as she pulled out of the driveway.

"I may have to," muttered Jody as the red car disappeared. She turned to Tom and said as diplomatically as she could, "Maybe we should walk."

Tom raised an eyebrow. "Don't you trust me? Besides, I thought you didn't want to be dull." He moved toward her, threatening to tickle her. "Come on, Jod, where's your sense of adventure?"

"Okay, okay." Jody wiggled away.

"This could be tricky, though."

"Impossible's more like it." Jody winced. "Maybe I should have just gone in the car."

"You sorry you stayed?" he asked quietly.

"No," Jody assured him. "Just a little scared."

"That's why I'm here." Tom gave her a comforting hug. His arms felt warm and secure. Her head fit snugly against his chest, and she could hear his heart beat. Jody closed her eyes and let herself sink into the sensation of closeness. It was better than anything she'd imagined, and she wished she could stay in his arms forever.

"Trust me," Tom whispered.

Jody leaned her head back and looked up at him. "With my life, it seems."

Tom met her gaze, his eyes turning an even darker blue, and for a moment Jody thought he might kiss her. Instead, he smiled and gently released her. "I guess I'll have to prove myself worthy of your trust," he said.

Tom leaned the bike against the Bauer's lamp-post, and then easily lifted Jody up by the waist and balanced her on the handlebar. When the bike started to wobble, Tom caught her, and Jody gave serious thought to losing her balance again. She reconsidered, figuring it would happen naturally anyway.

Tom got on behind her. "Hold on, here we go." With a heave-ho, he balanced the bike and pushed off. "We've got to pick up steam on this decline," he shouted as they pulled out of the drive. He pedaled faster as they wheeled through the neighborhood, past Marlie's house and the light on Thirty-fifth Avenue. Tom was really pedaling hard now.

"I'm too heavy," cried Jody. "Let's get off and walk."

"Nothing doing," puffed Tom. "This is a great workout for my legs. 'I think I can, I think I can, I think I can.' See, we're—puff—almost to—PUFF—the top of the hill."

"You made it," shouted Jody in genuine amazement as they reached the crest of the hill.

"*We* made it," corrected Tom. "Now hold on tight. Going down hill is even worse."

Jody wished she could cover her eyes. Instead she closed them tightly until Tom slowed down and coasted into Bittersweet Park.

It was a beautiful open park with rambling hills, even a running track around a lake. Jody spotted the group by a stand of evergreens.

"Over here," shouted Marlie.

"We're about to start a round of Frisbee golf," hollered Jeff through cupped hands.

Frisbee golf, Jody discovered, was similar to regular golf, but played in teams using a Frisbee instead of balls and clubs. Each team member would alternately take a turn tossing the Frisbee toward the next "hole" or obstacle.

Jeff jumped on top of their picnic table and announced the course for the first hole. "The Frisbee has to go around the left side of the barbecue, through the big V in the tree branches, around the right side of the fire hydrant, between the tires of Tom's bike, and finally land on top of Laura's picnic blanket. A par five," he bragged.

"All that in five throws?" Laura asked in disbelief.

Jeff draped an arm around her shoulder. "No

sweat, Laura, you've got me," he boasted. Jody almost sympathized with Laura.

"And don't forget that wherever the Frisbee lands is where the team has to stand for their next shot," Doug added, slipping his arm around Marlie's waist and claiming her as his partner.

"What do you say you and I team up," Tom asked Jody.

"Great," she agreed.

After all the teams were set, the competition began with much laughter and clowning around.

As the game progressed, the players' abilities began to surface. On the third hole, Jeff's tosses were great, but Laura's were all terrible. Marlie and Doug won the fifth hole with a great piggy-back shot by Marlie through the branches of a big tree. The hours of ultimate Frisbee that Jody's brothers had put her through proved to be an asset, keeping her team in the thick of the competition. Although Tom was a good athlete, he hadn't spent much time throwing a Frisbee, and he had a little trouble. Finally, he was faced with a tough last shot between the bench and the bottom of the tabletop. If he made this shot, Jody and Tom would beat Laura and Jeff and win the championship.

Jody took a deep breath and gave Tom an encouraging smile. They stood together on the spot where Jody's toss had landed. " 'I think I can, I think I can, I think I can,' " she gently repeated into Tom's ear.

"Go for it!" cheered Marlie.

"Here goes nothing," Tom said.

"You can say that again," grumbled Jeff.

Tom lowered himself to toss the Frisbee between the bench and the table. He took a deep breath and hurled the disk. It sailed over the bench and then crashed into the seat on the opposite side. Tom fell on the ground in frustration.

"Oh, too bad," said Marlie.

"Oh well, it's just a game," Jody said, taking Tom's hand. "It doesn't matter. That was a lot of fun, but now I'm starving. Let's get something to eat."

Tom didn't budge from the spot. He shook his head, looking almost angry. "I can't believe I blew it." By this time Jeff was prancing around singing the *Rocky* theme song, raising his arms triumphantly.

"Let's eat before I get sick," said Doug.

"Hey, don't feel bad, Arnold," Jeff taunted, "I heard that guys from Bradford weren't very athletic."

Doug was glaring at Jeff. "Very funny, Reynolds."

Lunch was awkward with Tom barely speaking, and Jody, Marlie, and Doug trying to cheer him up. Jeff didn't help much, either. He kept trying to put his arm around Jody's shoulders.

Laura and Jeff are a strange couple, Jody thought. *They've been going out for over a year, but they don't seem very happy.* The only thing that made sense about them was that they were a lot alike.

After lunch Jody packed up the cooler and took it to Marlie's car. She was glad to be by herself for a few moments and even stopped for a moment to admire the snowy range, miles off in the distance. Long's Peak looked gorgeous, she thought. Suddenly, someone jumped from behind the bushes and grabbed her around the waist. Tired of Jeff's games, Jody decided to teach him a lesson. Without looking, she caught his arm, shifted her weight to her left hip and flipped the jokester head over heels. Not until the culprit landed, did Jody realize she had flipped Tom instead.

"Wow, did you see that," howled Jeff, coming up behind them. "King Kong flips Fae Wray!"

"I'm so sorry," Jody said bending down to the gasping Tom. "I thought you were Jeff. Are you all right?" she asked, trying to help him up.

"I'm just fine," he said coldly, shrugging her off. "Never been better."

"Tom," Jody began, but she didn't know what to say.

"Bet you're a terror on the football field, Arnold." As usual Jeff didn't know when to stop teasing.

Tom had had enough. Without another word, he jumped up and headed for his bike.

"Forget him," Jeff told Jody. "He's embarrassed."

"I thought I was flipping *you*," Jody fired back. "Just leave me alone!"

Jody ran after Tom, but he had gone. She could feel the stinging tears rolling down her face. Not able to face anyone, she ran up the hill for home.

Chapter Eight

Jody checked the wood-grained clock that hung above the cupboard in the Bauers' kitchen. "Seven-thirteen P.M.," she grumbled.

"Ten minutes since the last time you looked," her mother observed. "You know the old saying, 'a watched pot never boils.'"

"I know," said Jody, dejectedly flipping another three cards in her solitaire game.

Her mother looked at her with concern. "You must have played over a hundred games of solitaire this weekend. What's wrong, honey?"

"Nothing, Mom, really." Jody gathered her cards. "I lost again."

"I think it's more than the cards. It's not like you to stay cooped up all weekend."

"Maybe I'm getting a bug." Jody placed her palm on her forehead.

"Maybe it's time for one of our famous hot chocolate chats."

"I'm not a little girl anymore, Mom."

"I know you're not," Jody's mother said calmly. "You know Grams and I still have our chats whenever we get together. Let's give it a try."

They'd started having these "chats" when Jody was little. Whenever she would get too quiet, her mother always knew she had something on her mind. Once it was a lost skate key. Lately, discussions had graduated to being left out of a party or not being chosen as a cheerleader. *How am I going to tell her about Tom?* Jody wondered as her mother plopped marshmallows in their cocoa.

"Did you ever beat Daddy?" Jody blurted out.

"If you mean have I ever hit your father, no," Mrs. Bauer said, crossing over to Jody and putting down the steamy mugs.

"No," Jody said with a chuckle. "I mean like in sports or school or something like that."

"Well, Daddy was always more athletic than I was, but that didn't mean I didn't try to 'beat him' as you put it."

"So you don't think I should hold back because I'm a girl?"

Mrs. Bauer stared into her cup. "It could depend on what the risk is. But as a general rule, your dad and I have always hoped you'd try your best. If that meant winning, we hoped you'd be gracious and kind."

Jody felt better about her prowess at Frisbee.

"Did something happen at the park with Tom?"

Jody looked at her mother, stunned. How could she have known about Tom and the park? Jody was sure she'd only mentioned Tom once or twice. *Am I that transparent?* she wondered.

The phone rang, and Jody nearly jumped out of her skin. "I'll get it," she cried. *Please be Tom*, she thought, running to the study to answer.

But Paul, who'd been in the den reading *Hot Rod,* beat her to it. "Bauer's residence," he drawled, picking up the phone. "Jody, no, I haven't seen her all day," he continued as Jody tried to grab the receiver. "Maybe you should call back later."

"Give me that phone," Jody pleaded, snatching it from his hand. "Hello," Jody practically screamed. "Oh, it's you." She sat down on the desk. "No, Marlie, I'm not sorry you called, I was just hoping it was, well, you know," Jody smiled shyly at her brother and turned away. Paul wandered out of the den, leaving the girls to their privacy.

"No, he hasn't called," Jody explained. "I know he never has before, but I thought after Saturday afternoon, he might. I keep imagining him flat on his back and gasping for air. How could I have done that?"

"It was an innocent mistake," Marlie assured her. "You thought it was Jeff."

"I wish it had been Jeff," Jody said, lying on the floor. "It's bad enough Tom missed the winning shot, but then to have Jeff watch me flip him." Her voice sounded shaky. "If Tom would just call, I'm sure we could work it out."

"Look, why don't you call him. That way you could apologize."

Jody sighed. "I apologized at the park. If I say I'm sorry again, it might be like adding salt to the wound."

"Well, just call him up to talk then," Marlie suggested.

"I can't." Jody sighed. "I know it's ridiculously old-fashioned, but I just can't. Besides, I've never called him before. I'd feel funny about starting that now."

"Okay," said Marlie, "but don't come crying to me if you don't hear from him."

"Thanks a lot, Marls," moaned Jody. "Look, let's make it short in case he does call. I'll see you tomorrow before English anyway."

Jody hung up slowly and dunked the last of her marshmallow with her index finger. Mrs. Bauer poked her head in the study door.

"Do you feel any better?" she asked.

"A little," Jody said, smiling. "I realize I didn't do anything wrong by doing my best. And, well, the other thing I apologized for, so there's nothing I can do. The ball is in his court." Jody tapped the desk with her mug. "In the meantime, I can't sit around here moping. It's getting kind of late, but I think I'll go out for a brisk walk. I could sure use the exercise."

"Want some company?" her mom said with a wink.

Jody laughed, unable to resist. "And when we get back, how about a mean game of gin? A penny a point."

For a few hours Sunday night Jody felt better, but by the time she tried to go to sleep, she was feeling "queasy" again.

At school on Monday Jody was so miserable her stomach ached. She ambled into history class and doodled on her page waiting for class to start.

" 'He flies through the air with the greatest of ease,' " Laura and Jeff were singing as they walked into class. "A Bradford boy without a trapeze."

Jody tried to block out their laughter.

"Hey, Jody," continued Jeff. "I told coach Martin about the flip, and he arranged a tryout for you for the wrestling team. How much do you weigh, anyway?"

Jody leapt to her feet and glared at him. "Why don't you just leave me alone?"

"Careful, Jeff, she might challenge you to an arm wrestling match," warned Laura.

The bell rang and everyone slowly sat down. "I hate Jeff Reynolds!" Jody scribbled on her paper. "And Laura Fielding, too!" She pressed so hard that the lead of her pencil broke. In disgust she got up and stomped to the sharpener. As she passed Marlie's desk, Marlie shoved a neatly folded note toward her. Jody quickly palmed the paper and sharpened her pencil. Back at her desk, Jody carefully unfolded the letter.

Sorry if I sounded insensitive last night. It's just that I feel so bad for you and wish I could help. Doug promised to let me know if he talks to Tom. Until then, I'm all ears. Please forgive me.

Your friend,

Marlie

P.S. Don't let Laura and Jeff bug you. They're not worth it!

Jody smiled and looked up. Mr. Freeman was looking at her suspiciously, so she jotted down a few notes.

No matter how hard she tried, Jody couldn't keep her mind off Tom and her dilemma. *I just wish I could talk to him,* she thought. She unfolded Marlie's note and reread it. Suddenly it hit her.

A letter, she thought as the inspiration came to her. *I'll send Tom a letter. That way I could communicate with him, without having to call him.* Jody flipped to the back of her notebook and took a piece of pale blue construction paper from her art class supplies. She creased it in half and began writing:

I'm so glad you're doing the play. It's giving me a chance to see how special you are. Thank you for the wonderful times we've had together. I hope we will have many more. I'm sorry if I caused you any embarrassment or pain.
Fondly,
Jody

She wanted to sign it "love, Jody," but knew that she couldn't. *You really are old-fashioned,* she thought to herself.

With a few folds of another piece of paper Jody constructed an envelope. Feeling hopeful for the first time in days, she rushed into the hall after class to tell Marlie.

"What do you think?" Jody asked after she'd explained her letter inspiration to Marlie.

"Great, but do you know his address?"

"No," Jody said glumly. "Plus it wouldn't get to him before rehearsal tonight, anyway. I guess it was a pretty stupid idea."

"Unless," Marlie said, "You take it over to Bradford and deliver it yourself."

"I can't let him see me!" Jody cried.

"No problem," Marlie said calmly. "We'll go in disguise.

Jody looked at her in disbelief. "You mean, we'll wear masks?"

"Not exactly. We can borrow some clothes from the costume room in the theater. We're supposed to try on some dresses, anyway, so I'm sure Mrs. French will lend us the key."

Marlie sounded so excited and sure of herself that Jody found herself quickly agreeing to the plan. The girls headed for the auditorium.

"I wonder where they get all this stuff," Jody said as she plopped a yellow pillbox hat on her head.

"Donations, I guess."

"Actually this isn't too bad," Jody said, modeling a wool tweed coat with large buttons and a fur collar. "That is, if you're a bag lady."

"Look at these," howled Marlie, tugging on a pair of men's black goulashes and topping them with a knee-length plaid kilt and an old marching band hat. The girls met in front of the mirror. After a moment of admiring silence, they both burst out laughing.

"Some disguise," said Jody.

"We'd be spotted in a second," agreed Marlie.

"Or arrested." Jody removed the pillbox hat. "I think our cover would definitely be uncovered."

After a few refinements the girls opted for floppy felt hats, long black trench coats, and sunglasses.

"This ought to do it," Jody said, flipping up her collar. "But how do we get out of classes to go? They'll know something is up if we both leave together."

"I've got it," said Marlie. "I told Mrs. French, I'd pick up the programs for her sometime today. Maybe she'll let me go now."

Jody shook her head. "That still doesn't solve the problem of getting past the pass-slip guard at the gate."

"I've got that figured out, too. You can ride in the trunk behind the backseat."

"You really have lost your mind," Jody said.

"Just trust me," Marlie said. "Meet me at the car in ten minutes."

"This is crazy," Jody announced, locking the door of the costume room. "Love has driven me to riding in the trunk, dressing like Double-O-Seven, and sending secret letters."

"Just do it," Marlie ordered and left, heading for Mrs. French's room.

"I can't breathe in here," Jody yelled from the trunk of Marlie's car. "I think I'm getting claustrophobia."

"Be quiet, or we'll never get away with it," Marlie yelled back.

"What if I sneeze?"

"You'll make me laugh, and then I'll pop the clutch and you'll pop out of the back."

Both girls tried to be serious, but the whole situation was giving them the giggles. Marlie ended up driving around the parking lot three times before they drove toward the pass guard.

"Quiet," Marlie called, "we're almost there. You want to deliver that card, don't you?"

Marlie slowly came to a stop, rolled down her window, and showed the parking guard her slip from Mrs. French. He gave a quick look in the backseat and then waved them on their way. Marlie hit the gas, accidentally popping the clutch in her excitement. Seconds later Jody smacked up against the backseat flap, a tangle of arms and legs. Laughing hysterically, she jumped out of the back and crawled into the front seat.

Jody and Marlie arrived at Bradford during lunch. They mingled with the crowds unnoticed, they hoped. As they walked by the auditorium Jody remembered the last time she had been in those halls—the day of the auditions when she first met Tom. They went up the same stairway, hoping to see him at his locker.

"There's a billion lockers up here," Marlie complained. "We're never going to find his."

"All I know is that it's on the second floor. He's bound to stop there during lunch."

They zigzagged their way onto the second floor, trying to remain inconspicuous.

"Jody, we're the only ones up here wearing coats, hats, and sunglasses," Marlie observed. "Maybe this was a bad idea."

Jody tried to keep a straight face. "It was your idea, and we're too far into it to stop now. Just keep your eyes peeled for Tom."

"If Doug sees me, I'll die. At least take the sunglasses off," Marlie pleaded, sticking hers in her purse.

"Here," Jody said, handing her the glasses. Just then the bell rang, and students poured through the halls. Marlie turned red and pulled her hat over her eyes.

"I think I see him," Jody said tugging on Marlie's jacket. "Come on." They ducked into an alcove.

"It's him," Jody whispered. "He's at his locker. It's directly across from the hall light."

"And the window," added Marlie, maneuvering around Jody to get a better view. A few moments later Tom was gone, and Jody was ready to make her move.

She tiptoed down the empty hallway and made it to the locker. "Number Fifty-two," she whispered to herself. Jody held the note close to her heart and made a wish. *Please let Tom forgive me. I'll just die if he never talks to me again.* Leaving a corner of the envelope showing through the locker slats, Jody darted back to the alcove.

"Fancy meeting you here," Doug said, surprising Jody as she walked up to Marlie.

"He saw us the minute we came on the second floor," Marlie explained with a moan.

"You won't tell Tom," Jody pleaded.

Doug crossed his arms over his chest. "On one condition."

"Name it, anything, just please don't tell him I'm here."

"Let me steal Marlie from you for ten minutes. And one more thing."

"What?"

Doug grinned at her. "Take off that stupid hat."

"I kind of liked it," Jody said, stuffing it under her arm.

"I'll meet you at the car in ten minutes. Okay, Jod?" Marlie called over her shoulder, already halfway down the hall.

"Fine," Jody answered, leaning against the wall, relieved to have delivered her letter without any problems. She poked her head around the corner to double-check. The card was still there, and Tom was walking toward his locker again. But before he could reach it a pretty redheaded girl stopped him. Jody couldn't hear what they were talking about, but what she saw didn't leave room for much doubt. They talked easily; obviously they knew each other well. Then Tom took the girl's hand, and she gave him a big hug.

What a fool I've been, Jody thought miserably. *He already has a girlfriend. That's why he's never called or asked me out, or tried to kiss me. How stupid could I be?* Then she gasped aloud as she remembered. *Oh, no. The card! I've got to get that card back*, she thought frantically.

Cautiously, she peered around the corner again. As soon as she saw that the coast was clear, she ran to the locker. With the skill of a brain surgeon, she gently tugged on the corner of the envelope. But it wouldn't budge. She tugged some more, and the envelope fell—all the way in. Giving the locker a resounding kick, Jody ran downstairs to wait for Marlie.

Chapter Nine

That night at rehearsal Jody purposely avoided Tom.

"You're being really silly," Marlie lectured. "Doug told me Tom doesn't have a girlfriend at Bradford. Besides if he read your card, you two should finally talk and resolve things."

"There is nothing to resolve," Jody stated.

"How do you know unless you talk to him? Promise me you'll at least see him."

"I'll do no such thing," Jody said, stretching out. "If he read that note he can come to me. I'm not throwing myself at him anymore. I swear, Marlie, boys are the weirdest creatures."

"What makes you say that?"

Marlie's sarcasm was lost on Jody who angrily answered the question. "First I found out Jeff's not what I thought he was, then Tom seems to have a girlfriend, and now to top it off, that nerd Ed Hooks, from Bradford, has been following me around all night long."

"Is that the guy that bought you a soda during the break?"

"Yes, and practically held my hand during that first note session. I just want to go home and think about becoming a nun."

Marlie patted her shoulder sympathetically. "It's not that bad, but I'll tell you what. If it would help, I'll say good-bye to Doug right after notes, and we'll go home fast, okay?"

"The sooner the better," Jody muttered.

The rest of the evening went slowly. Jody made no attempt to even look at Tom, although according to Marlie he tried several times to catch her attention. Jody was too upset to notice. She was having enough trouble with Ed, and he insisted on walking her to the parking lot.

"It really made my day when I got your card, Jody," Ed explained as they reached Marlie's car.

"M-My card?" Jody stammered.

Ed reached down and squeezed her hand. "I had no idea you felt that way, but I'm glad you do."

"Ed," Jody said with a sinking feeling, "you've got to tell me something. What's your locker number?"

"Fifty-two."

"Oh, well, Ed," Jody tried to think quickly. She didn't want to hurt his feelings. "I just think you're doing a great job as the mayor in the play and I thought you should know."

"Sorry to break this up," Marlie said, rushing in, "but I've got to get home."

"Good night, Ed," Jody said, gratefully sliding into the car. She waited until they'd left the school grounds before she spoke again. And when she did she was on the verge of tears. "Oh, Marlie, Tom never got the card. Ed did. Tom still doesn't know how I feel, and what if Doug's wrong and he *does* have a girlfriend? What am I going to do?"

"I've lost Tom," Jody told Marlie the next day as they touched up their makeup after gym class. "He didn't even say hi last night at rehearsal."

Marlie brushed on some blush. "Did you try talking to him?"

"No, but, he's the one who stormed off."

"You're going to let that stop you from getting back together?"

"I don't know." Jody sighed, adding a touch of teal blue eye shadow. "I'm so confused, I'm not even sure we were together."

"But you're still nuts about him, right?"

"More than ever."

"Okay," Marlie said, giving her hair a final brush. "You just need to work out another plan. One that gets you talking again. Maybe we'll figure something out while we unload chairs. Now hurry up and dry your hair."

"Unload chairs? What do you mean 'unload chairs'?"

"Remember, we promised Mrs. French that we'd unload the orchestra folding chairs from Bradford today during lunch."

"*We* promised?" Jody echoed. "*We* didn't volunteer us. *You* volunteered us."

Marlie picked up her bag and started out the door. "Just dry your hair and come on."

"Who cares if my hair is wet? I'm just doing manual labor. I don't have to look good to do that."

"Suit yourself," Marlie said, looking at her watch, "but don't forget I warned you."

"All right, all right," Jody grumbled, picking up her books. "This is turning out to be a lousy week."

Marlie threw Jody her flannel-lined jean jacket and practically pushed her up the concrete steps of the spacious gymnasium. "Hurry up," she urged. "We'll be late."

"Who cares, and since when did you get so eager?" Jody yelled as they wheeled around the halls toward the auditorium loading dock. "You know this is probably my social event for the year."

"Quit complaining," Marlie said, opening the auditorium door.

"I'm probably the only sophomore girl who has never been on a date," Jody stated as they slowed down. "Worse, my sixteenth birthday is coming up, and I've never had a real kiss. I finally meet someone who seems sincere and what do I do but publicly humiliate him."

"Would you quit cutting yourself down! Tom still cares about you. You just need to get back on track. So, comb your hair and let's find the truck."

"What does my hair have to do with it," Jody muttered.

The girls went down the backstage steps of the auditorium to where the double doors of the truck were open. "You go ahead and start, Jod. I'll tell Mrs. French we're here."

"Somehow I'm getting the short end of the straw," Jody grumbled to herself as she stepped onto the truck. Stacks of folding chairs reached almost to the ceiling. And suddenly next to the first stack of chairs Jody spied a familiar pair of tennis shoes. She slowly looked up past the jeans and red-and-black sweatshirt to Tom's warm smile.

"I know you're pretty strong," he said. "But would you like some help with those chairs?"

"I'm so sorry about flipping you," Jody blurted out.

"I shouldn't have let Jeff get to me," Tom said at the same time.

"I wanted to call," they said in unison, and both of them began laughing.

"Maybe we should take turns," Tom suggested with a grin.

Jody took a deep breath. "Jeff was bugging me so much that day. I assumed it was him when I flipped *you*."

"And I felt so bad about blowing the last shot in the Frisbee game," Tom confessed. "That's what happens when I try to be Mr. Macho. After Jeff started with the charm and you flipped me, I figured I should cut my losses and leave. I'm sorry, too," he said gently. "I should have realized what he was doing."

"Look, if we finish this unloading pretty fast, maybe we can get a pizza before Tom and I have to get the truck back to Bradford," said Doug's voice behind them. "After all, this is our lunch hour."

Jody turned to see Doug and Marlie smiling behind her. "Don't be mad," Marlie said, "I just couldn't stand to see you so unhappy."

"Tom was acting the same way," Doug added.

"So we figured we'd get you together and you could at least talk."

"You and I are free from now through study hall, so we could go for pizza, and we won't miss any classes," Marlie pointed out.

"Is it a date then, Jody?" Tom asked.

"A date," Jody repeated, dazzled. "Sure! Oh, no! My hair," she moaned.

"I tried to tell you," Marlie said, laughing.

Tom ran a hand through her damp hair. "It looks fine."

"Let's get moving," Doug ordered, sounding like a drill sergeant. "I'm starved!"

Tom then organized them into an assembly line. He passed the chairs to Jody, who handed them to Marlie inside the theater, who then gave them to Doug to set up inside the orchestra pit.

The plan worked beautifully, and they soon were going at a quick-paced rhythm. Every once in a while when Tom handed her a chair, their hands would touch. Jody tried to act nonchalant, but each time it happened her skin would tingle. She wondered if Tom had the same feeling. During school, she had watched other couples holding hands as they walked to their classes. Now, she imagined Tom holding her hand and escorting her to English or math.

Forty-five minutes later the chairs were set

up and ready for the night's first run-through with full orchestra, and the foursome headed for Cables End Pizzeria.

"I'm so hungry my stomach started growling a half hour ago," Doug moaned.

"I dreamed of pepperoni and onions every time I carried another chair," Jody said.

"Topped with extra cheese," Marlie continued.

"And, of course, gallons of anchovies," Tom added.

"Anchovies?" the others shouted in disgust.

"Yeah, I always get extra anchovies, don't you?"

Doug groaned. "I'll tell you what, Arnold," he said as he turned his car into the restaurant parking lot. "You and Jody find a place to sit, and Marlie and I will order the pizza, minus the anchovies."

Tom gave Doug a withering glare and then got out of the truck and offered his arm to Jody.

"How's this look?" he asked as they approached a corner booth.

"Perfect," Jody answered, taking off her jacket and slipping into the seat. She hadn't felt so happy since they'd gone kite flying.

"I'm really glad Doug talked me into coming with him today," Tom said quietly. "When you didn't talk to me at last night's rehearsal, I figured I was a goner."

124

Jody looked at him in surprise. "What do you mean?"

"Well, usually we at least talk at rehearsal. Last night you didn't even look at me." Tom leaned forward and stared at the table. "I figured you were too embarrassed to be seen with me."

"I can't believe you thought that," Jody said apologetically. "I must have looked like a real snob. You see, I really felt awful after the flipping incident. I guess having two brothers on the wrestling team has its disadvantages." She leaned back in the booth and shrugged. "They used to like to practice their moves on me. I finally got tired of the bruises, so I watched them enough to learn how to retaliate. That flip is the only move I know, but I guess it works."

"Oh, it works all right," Tom said, rubbing the back of his head.

Jody grinned but went on with her explanation. "After the weekend I was still feeling pretty bad about everything, and I couldn't wait until rehearsal to tell you. So I stuck a card in your locker."

"I never got a card," Tom said with a frown.

"I know," Jody moaned. "I found out at last night's rehearsal that I'd put it in the wrong locker. Ed Hooks thought I was chasing him."

Tom's blue eyes were dancing with amusement. "That's pretty funny, but I had no idea all this was going on. How'd you even know which locker was mine?"

"Well, obviously, I didn't. All I knew was that it was on the second floor. Then I took an educated guess when I saw you standing there with your—er—redhead."

"My redhead?"

Jody shrugged. "She looked like somebody you knew very well."

"I don't think I know any redheads," said Tom, sounding puzzled. "Are you sure?"

"Well, I hardly noticed, but she seemed to be about five foot four, reddish hair, wearing a light blue sweater and a black skirt. I think you knew her." Jody's voice was quiet and unsure. "I wasn't trying to spy, but I did see you hug her."

"I can't think of who you're talking about," Tom began. "Wait a minute. You must mean Jeanne."

"She must be someone special." Jody tried to sound casual.

"She is," Tom said. "But not in the way you mean. I've known her since I was three years old."

"Really?" Jody said, beginning to feel hopeful again.

"She's running for student body secretary this

spring, and she asked me to be her campaign manager. I told her 'sure.' So you must have seen her giving me a thank-you hug."

"Is that all?" Jody asked.

"Honest, Jeanne is like a sister." Tom paused for a minute, and his dimple widened as he grinned. "You thought we were dating, and that's why you didn't talk to me at rehearsal?" Tom took her hands from across the table and held them tightly in his own. "Look, before Doug and Marlie come back, there's something I want to tell you. I really like you, Jody. I know it's hard since we go to different schools, but I'll get my driver's license soon, and then we'll spend more time together. Meanwhile, let's make the most of our time at rehearsals, okay?"

"Okay," Jody answered, her voice trembling with excitement. "I—I really like you, too." She wanted to scream the news to everyone and never wanted to let go of Tom's hands. *This is the best day of my life*, she thought, gazing into his blue eyes and feeling warm all over.

Chapter Ten

Later that afternoon Jody rushed to her three o'clock orthodontist's appointment. She was sorry to miss the special afternoon rehearsal and costume check since Tom would be there, but she was still nine feet off the ground because she'd finally worked things out with him.

Dr. Wynn's office was small but comfortable and familiar to Jody. Everywhere she looked she saw pictures of people smiling. Big smiles, little smiles, toothy smiles, and tons of faces with braces. There were two pictures side by side that Jody always looked at when she came. A young girl's before and after shots. Her teeth were gorgeous and her smile stunning. Jody knew that someday she would feel it was worth having braces. But it was the "when" that was getting her down. She didn't blame a boy for not wanting to kiss a metal mouth, but how much longer could she stand to wait for her first kiss? Especially now that she had someone special to give her that kiss.

Dr. Wynn called her into his office, and Jody slid into the large, gray couch-chair. She closed her eyes and wrinkled her nose at the smell. She had thought she'd get used to that medicinal smell, but she never had.

"How's the play going?" Dr. Wynn asked as he checked Jody's mouth. "Do you think you'll be ready to open this weekend?"

"I hope so," Jody tried to answer without biting off his fingers. *Why does he always ask me questions when his hands are in my mouth?* she thought irritably.

"Are you getting attached to these things?" asked Dr. Wynn, tapping the metal. "Or do you think you'd like to get rid of them?"

"What?" Jody answered, unprepared.

"These braces are coming off."

"When?" Jody tried not to scream.

"Right now, if it's a good time for you," he said with a grin.

"Right now is great!"

"I wanted to tell you on your last appointment," he explained, "but I didn't want to get your hopes up if that molar didn't adjust."

"I can't believe it." Jody sighed.

"You'll still have to have a few more visits and

wear retainers, but at least you'll see your teeth again. This procedure might hurt a bit, but then they're gone forever."

Jody was too excited to worry about pain. Whenever she felt a twinge, she thought about Tom and her first kiss.

Dr. Wynn started clipping the wires, and Jody imagined what her teeth would look like. *Maybe Tom was waiting for me to get my braces off before he kissed me*, she thought and instantly knew it wasn't true. Tom was different; she knew he cared about her.

After about an hour of pounding and clipping, Jody's mouth ached. Dr. Wynn handed her a mirror. "Well, what do you think?"

Jody smiled and saw a mountain range of white teeth. "They look so big and feel so slippery," she said a little frightened.

"You just haven't seen them for a while. They'll look normal to you in a day or so."

"I love them already," Jody said, beginning to feel very good about her new look. She ran her tongue over her now-smooth teeth. "Thank you so much." She hopped off the chair, flaunted her new smile to everyone in the office, and ran the quarter of a mile home.

Jody carefully picked out her outfit to wear to that night's rehearsal. She knew she'd be wearing her costume once they started, but she wanted to wear something to show off her new smile. She french-braided her hair and put on just the right amount of makeup. Every few minutes she would run to the mirror and stare and giggle and jump up and down. By the time she heard Marlie's horn she was ready to make her entrance.

"Wait till you see my costume," Marlie announced as Jody got into the car.

"Thanks again for helping us get back together today," Jody said with an exaggerated smile.

"Anytime. Besides you were a pain to be around."

"Sorry," Jody said, flashing her teeth again.

"I can't believe the show opens this weekend. I'm so nervous."

"So am I," Jody said, giving up. She was quiet for the rest of the trip, but her excitement grew again as they drew near the school.

"Nice dress," Doug said to her as she and Marlie walked into the auditorium.

"And you've got to show me how to do that to my hair," one of the dancers stated.

Marlie looked at her and frowned. "You look different. I know what it is. You've never worn those boots before."

Jody couldn't believe no one had noticed her teeth.

"Wait a minute," Marlie said, looking carefully. "Turn around once very slowly."

Jody did so, smiling naturally.

"Oh, my goodness," Marlie said, "you got your braces off!"

"Right," Jody cheered.

"Your teeth look beautiful," Marlie cried, hugging Jody. Suddenly Jody was surrounded.

"They're so straight," said Doug.

"They'd better be," Jody answered.

Jeff reached out and squeezed her shoulder. "Now you'll have to find a new way to sparkle onstage," he said.

Jody briefly considered flipping him, but Mrs. French's voice broke in. "Everyone in costume and ready to go in five minutes."

I'll have to show Tom later, Jody thought. *Since I missed this afternoon's costume check, I'd better try on my costume now.*

Jody soon discovered that Dr. Wynn's work had indeed been noticed. Lots of the kids mentioned it, telling her she looked great. During the first-act break, while she had to stand still for costume adjustments, Ed Hooks approached her. "Hey Jody," he whispered. "I'd love to drive you home after rehearsal."

"No thank you," Jody answered quickly.

Jody concentrated on her third-act dance number. She practically forgot all about her teeth until just before her love scene with Jeff.

"How about going to the opening-night party with me," Jeff asked her in the wings. "We'd be the best-looking couple there."

"No thanks," Jody told him. "And it's a cast party. Everyone is invited."

When Jeff started to kiss her on the lips during their scene for the first time, Jody quickly turned her head. *This is supposed to be a glorious moment,* she thought. Instead, she was crushed with frustration and insecurity.

"Did Tom ask you out?" Marlie asked later as they changed out of their costumes and got ready to go home.

"I still haven't talked to him tonight," Jody admitted. "What if he only likes me for my teeth?"

"Don't be stupid," Marlie said. "He liked you this afternoon when you still had your braces."

"You're right," Jody said, putting on her own clothes. "But I feel scared."

Marlie shook her head sympathetically and headed for the door. "I'm going to find Doug, so I'll see you at the car. Relax and find Tom."

Finding Tom was easier than Jody expected. He was waiting for her right outside the dressing room.

He smiled at her, and she hesitantly returned the smile. "I had a great time at lunch today," he said.

"Me, too," Jody answered quietly.

"I'm glad we got things cleared up."

"It was awful going to rehearsal and not talking to you," Jody admitted.

Tom grinned. "I know. I think Doug was ready to shoot me. I kept spending the breaks talking to him, and all he wanted to do was talk to Marlie."

Jody couldn't figure out why Tom hadn't said anything about her teeth, but she felt strangely relieved. Together they walked out of the school.

"I was watching you from the wings," Tom said. "You looked really good tonight." He took her hand. "Both on- and offstage."

"Thanks," Jody said, feeling suddenly shy. "Your songs went well, too. Are you excited about opening night?"

"Yeah, but I'm glad it's still a few days away."

"Me, too, I can sure use the rehearsal time."

Jody thought the conversation was going very safely when Tom changed the subject. "You caused quite a stir with your new smile tonight," he said. In the darkness it was hard to tell whether or not he was teasing her.

"Oh, it's not such a big deal," she replied,

trying to shrug if off but feeling her heart beating fast.

"Well"—Tom took both of Jody's hands so that she was facing him—"I always thought your smile was pretty. Now it's even prettier."

"Oh, thank you!" Jody cried as all the night's tension flowed out of her. Without even thinking, she threw her arms around his shoulders and hugged him.

"You don't think they're too big, do you?" she asked, unconsciously pulling away.

"What are too big?" Tom asked.

"My teeth."

Tom put his arm around Jody's shoulders and gave her a hug. "I think they look terrific, but that's completely beside the point."

"What do you mean?"

"I mean," Tom said, "that your teeth look great, but that doesn't really matter. With or without your braces, Jody Bauer, I'm crazy about you."

Chapter Eleven

On opening night Jody's stomach was doing flip-flops, handsprings, and Russian splits. *Too bad I'm not trying out for cheerleader,* she thought, *my stomach would be sure to win. So, this is what they mean by opening night jitters.*

Jody was at the theater two hours early. She sat in one of the seats in the audience and imagined watching herself onstage. She had become more self-assured in the past two months. It wasn't just doing the show, or getting her braces off, not even Tom. Being cast had made her feel a part of the school, that first drop in the bucket. It was all part of becoming Jody and she liked it.

Slowly she got up from the chair and crossed the bridge on stage where she would dance over the pot of gold, then with a twirl to the empty auditorium, she went to her dressing room.

The dressing room was, of course, empty. Jody sat alone in front of the mirror. "What if I fall on my face?" she said aloud, staring blankly. "I'd be too embarrassed to look at anyone again, not to mention Tom. Stop it!" she scolded her reflection. "You've worked hard, you won't fall on your face. You'll fall on the other end instead. So get to work!" Laughing, she looked at her new smile and went into action.

On the dressing room table, she laid out her favorite royal blue towel, a little mirror, and her makeup. Then Jody remembered the final touch; Mrs. French had suggested that all the cast bring "a little something from home to personalize your makeup space. Something to calm or encourage you," the director had said.

Jody carefully took out the dried flowers she and Tom had gathered the day they went kite flying. "Who would ever think that three cattails, two pussywillows, and a milkweed stalk, could be so special?" Jody said aloud. *I guess it's because Tom's so special*, she answered silently. Jody secured the bundle with a tiny piece of peach satin ribbon and stood the flowers gently against the mirror.

Jody pictured Tom onstage. He was so good in the show. When he sang his solo lines, his rich baritone voice rang out to every corner of the theater. Just thinking about it made her happy. She wondered if the other girls noticed how she felt. *Besides Laura, of course,* she thought. *Laura flirts with every guy.*

The night before Tom had said he had something to give Jody for good luck, but when they met after rehearsal Laura had grabbed him by the arm and asked him to help out backstage. Now, he'd asked Jody to meet him before the show. "Laura won't interfere this time," Jody vowed aloud.

"Jody, are you back here?" shouted Marlie from down the hall. The dressing room door opened and Marlie bounded in. "What are you doing, anyway," she asked. "Daydreaming?"

"What else," Jody answered with a grin.

"About Tom?" Marlie set her makeup on the table.

"Who else?"

"I just saw Doug out front, parking his car. Now I think we're the only ones here. Are you as nervous as I am?" Marlie rambled on as she twisted a lock of her blond hair.

"Petrified." Jody giggled. The girls clasped hands. "Everything has to be perfect."

"It will be," Marlie reassured her. "Unless" —she took a step back and wrinkled her nose—

"unless you're planning to wear *that* to the opening night party."

"What?" Jody asked, posing. "You mean to tell me I don't look *très chic* in this ensemble?" She twirled around and began strutting through the dressing room like a model. She was wearing her father's old dark green jumpsuit.

"Has Tom ever seen this side of you?" Marlie asked, amused.

"No way, I'd rather die first." She dropped the act and went to the clothes rack. "I brought my new cashmere green sweater for the party. I figured the green color was good luck for an Irish musical. Plus—" Jody held up a pair of green shoes that matched her sweater perfectly. They had a medium heel, scalloped sides, and gold flecks in the material.

"Fabulous," Marlie said, taking them from Jody and trying them on.

"I'm going to be doing chores for at least a month to pay my mom back, but tonight's special. How about you? What are you wearing?"

"I thought you'd never ask," Marlie said. "Tahdah!" She unbuttoned her coat and revealed black pants, a white long-sleeved ruffled blouse, and a black pleated vest that accentuated her tiny waistline. And to top it off, a black bow tie and black high heels with little bows in the back.

140

Jody imitated a wolf whistle as well as she could.

"I can't decide between the gold dangling earrings or the little black buttons." Marlie held one up to each ear. "What do you think?"

"I think you look incredible either way. How'd you come up with an idea like this?" Jody said, slowly circling Marlie.

"Well, Doug says all the orchestra members wear tuxes for the show, so I thought it might be kind of cute."

"Cute?" Jody said. "Sexy's more like it."

"I hope Doug likes it. Guess what?" Marlie hesitated. "Doug asked me to go steady last night."

"What did you say?" Jody asked.

"I said yes."

"That's great," Jody said, giving her friend a hug. "I'm so happy for you."

"Me, too." Marlie sighed as she waltzed around the room. "Hey." Marlie stopped dead in her tracks. "What was it Tom wanted to give you after the rehearsal yesterday?"

"Nothing," muttered Jody. "Absolutely nothing."

"He seemed so determined."

"I thought so, too," Jody said sitting back in her chair. "Until Laura showed up."

"Her again. She just loves attention. It seems

every time you and Tom have a few minutes together, she barges in."

"Tell me something I don't know," said Jody, leaning her chair on its back legs. "She just wants what she doesn't have. Every time she and Jeff have a tiff, she tries to make him jealous by flirting with Tom."

"All right, then." Marlie snapped her fingers. "It's time for a plan."

"What kind of plan?"

"Some kind of signal," Marlie said, tapping her nails on the table.

"What good is that going to do?"

Marlie began to pace. The wheels were beginning to roll. "I've got it. Whenever you and Tom have a chance to be alone, start whistling."

"Whistling?"

"Getting your braces off didn't ruin that, did it?"

"Of course not, but what should I whistle?"

Both girls passed each other pacing.

"How about 'If This Isn't Love' from the show?" said Jody.

"Perfect, I'll hear you whistle, find Laura, ask her about the party tonight, and keep her busy for a while."

"You know, Marlie, it just might work."

"Of course it'll work. I thought of it, didn't I?"

At that moment Laura burst into the dressing room, talking about the event of the year, the opening night party at her house. She was carrying an armful of cards and flowers.

I'm just going to ignore her, and that'll bug her the most, Jody thought. With a cool nod and a smile, the girls sealed their plan and went to the makeup table where each girl had a small space, to prepare for the show.

In order for Jody to see herself in the mirror, she had to move two of Laura's floral arrangements from her own section. She put on her base, blush, and lipstick. Laura was still flitting around the room, talking gibberish and posting cards on the wall. Jody smiled calmly and began brushing her hair. She reached for the other half of the peach ribbon she'd brought to wrap around her pigtails.

"They're gone!" Jody jumped to her feet. "My flowers are gone!" Frantically she searched the table for her treasure. "What have you done with my flowers?" she demanded as she whirled Laura around.

Laura barely looked at her. "What flowers?"

"The dried flowers with the peach ribbon." Jody slowly articulated each syllable.

"You mean those dead old things?"

"What did you do with them?" Jody repeated.

"I threw them out."

"What? You had no right!" Jody cried, rushing to the wastebasket.

"I thought I was being very generous sharing my beautiful *live* flowers with you."

"Well, next time don't do me any favors," Jody snapped, retrieving her bundle from the trash.

Sitting in her dressing area, Jody tried to tidy her crumpled flowers. The milkweed stalk was broken, and hanging by a thread. Carefully, she picked up the other half of the peach ribbon and used it like a bandage to wrap the stem. After a little kiss for better healing, she returned the bouquet to its original position. At once she felt better. Nothing, she decided, not even Laura could bother her now.

A final pat of powder and a snap of her calico dress, and Jody was ready to begin the show. She caught Marlie's attention and mimed whistling before sneaking out the door to find Tom. Looking down the hall, she saw him outside the green room, the room where actors wait for their entrances. He was also in costume—dark pants and vest, a yellow western shirt, and a cowboy hat.

"Hey, sheriff," Jody said. "where's your badge?"

"I'm having trouble with the clasp," Tom replied. "Think you might be able to help?"

"I'll give it a try." Jody took the badge from him and lifted up his vest to see if she could pin it on. Being close to him made her heart beat faster; she hoped she wouldn't start blushing.

"This is nice," Tom murmured. "I should have asked you to help me more often." Jody cocked her head and blushed. Tom slowly tilted his head toward Jody's.

"Hey, don't forget your holster," interrupted Ed. "We can't have a sheriff without a gun."

Jody and Tom jumped back and Jody straightened her hair.

"Right, Ed, uh, thanks." Tom took the gun belt from him.

"Let's see if we can find a quiet place," Tom said.

Immediately Jody started to loudly whistle "If This Isn't Love," hoping Marlie would pick up on her cue. Tom took her hand and they headed for the balcony door.

"Who's whistling?" shrieked Mrs. French. "I hear whistling backstage!" She marched over to Tom and Jody. "Don't you know whistling backstage is bad luck?"

"Well, I—" stammered Jody. "You said talking about *Macbeth* backstage was bad luck, but you never mentioned whistling was a jinx."

"Ahhh," wailed Mrs. French, "two bad omens." Before Jody could say another word, Mrs. French whisked her away from Tom. "We'll have to remedy this but quick." The next thing Jody knew, Mrs. French was leading her back through the green room toward the exit. Jody turned briefly to see Tom glued in place with his mouth gaping open.

"Turn around three times," Mrs. French ordered quickly as they stepped into the cold air.

'Huh?" Jody said, shivering.

"Quickly turn around three times." Jody did so. "Now spit," Mrs. French ordered.

"What?" Jody wondered if Mrs. French had lost her mind.

"Spit, it's all a part of the tradition. You don't want to spoil the show, do you?"

Jody spit feebly into the grass. "Gross," she mumbled.

Mrs. French nodded approvingly. "Now that takes care of the whistling. Repeat it again to the left to get rid of the hex caused by saying the title of that Scottish tragedy." Jody was too cold and frustrated to argue. She repeated her action and then followed Mrs. French back into the theater, mumbling under her breath about "stupid superstitions." She had to find Tom, but by the time she reached the balcony entrance, he was gone, and Mrs. French was in the green room collecting the cast for a final pep talk.

"Gather around, please; form a circle and join

hands," Mrs. French ordered. With a sigh, Jody joined the circle. When Tom came from behind and took Jody's right hand, she tried to listen to Mrs. French's encouraging words, but her heart was focused on Tom. She only had to look at him to feel warm and secure. No matter how nervous she was about the performance, she felt strong as long as Tom was holding her hand.

"Let the energy bonding this circle seal the feeling of togetherness it takes to have a successful show," Mrs. French chanted. "Take that energy to the stage with you. Now before we start, make a wish, squeeze the hands you're holding, and have fun and a wonderful show."

Jody hoped she would give the performance of her life. Her family wouldn't see the show until the next night. Tonight she wanted Tom to be proud of her.

"You'll be wonderful" Tom whispered as if sensing her thoughts. "You always are."

"Break a leg," Jody whispered back, using the old theater code for good luck.

"Promise to meet me immediately after the show?" Tom asked, giving Jody's hand a squeeze. Jody nodded, made her wish, gave Tom's hand another squeeze, and then let go.

The play went even better than anyone had hoped. Tom sang his solo lines beautifully, and

Jody's dances were received with thunderous applause. Except for one of the dancers turning the wrong way during the second act opening number, everything was perfect. A real feeling of accomplishment and togetherness flowed through Jody. Now if she could just get through the love scene with Jeff.

Jeff seemed more nervous than ever when it came time for the kiss. Jody had already decided not to move her head away if he was going to really kiss her. *It is just a stage kiss*, Jody thought, *but still . . .*

The time had come, and Jeff slowly bent toward Jody. His lips pressed against hers. She popped open her eyes when she felt nothing. NOTHING. His lips weren't soft or giving. It actually felt awful. *Is this what it's like being kissed?* she wondered. *Is this what I've been waiting fifteen and a half years for? What's the big deal?*

After the show, Jody tried to find Tom. But with so much excitement backstage, the harder she tried, the more difficult it became to get through the crowd.

"You were marvelous, Jody, really superb," Mrs. French told her.

"Great job, Jody." Jody turned to see Laura. "You were wonderful."

"That compliment means a lot," Jody said

sincerely. "I wanted to do your choreography justice."

"You really sparkled," said Doug, recalling Jeff's earlier comment.

Jody was overwhelmed by the response and gave in to the excitement. Across the room she saw Tom receiving the same accolades; he sent her an understanding glance and called out, "Ten minutes," pointing to the wall clock.

"Stage left," Jody called back.

"Did you hear *my* applause when we took our final bows?" Jeff swung Jody around. She just laughed and rushed to the dressing room.

Jody gave herself a quick check in the mirror. Ten minutes was not long enough to get ready for the party. She started to scrape off the layers of makeup and redo her hair.

"Did you meet Tom?" Marlie poked her head in the door.

"Not yet, I'm supposed to meet him—in four minutes," Jody moaned, looking at her watch.

"You'd better change quickly, then."

"I thought I'd meet him in my costume."

"You can't," Marlie said, coming into the dressing room. "They're picking up our outfits to be locked up for the night."

"What am I going to do? I can't get into my party clothes in three minutes flat."

"Well, it's the 'drab suit,' then."

"Get serious," said Jody slipping out of her costume.

"Go bare then," Marlie suggested with a grin. "I'm sure he'll never forget that."

"I'll just have to put my coat over this silly outfit," Jody said, snapping on the jumpsuit. Marlie handed her her shoes and overcoat, and Jody bounded out the door.

"Good luck!" Marlie shouted.

Jody rushed to stage left, hoping she hadn't missed Tom. But Tom wasn't in sight. She relaxed, took out a hand mirror, and continued to work on her hair. Five minutes later, still no Tom. "What could be keeping him?" she wondered out loud. "Maybe he's changing, too." After ten minutes of pacing, Jody considered going to look for him. But then they might miss each other. Her imagination started to go haywire as she wondered if Tom thought the crowd was more important than she was. After twenty minutes, she couldn't wait any longer, she *had* to find him.

In the hall Jody ran into Marlie. "Have you seen Tom?" she asked desperately.

"Everybody has left. Didn't you guys find each other?"

"He didn't show, and I'm worried. Have you seen him?"

"Yeah," Marlie slowly admitted.

"Well, where is he?"

"I just saw him loaded down with flowers, following Laura to the parking lot."

"I don't believe this," Jody said as she hit her head with the palm of her hand.

"She must have lassoed him into it."

Furious with Laura, Jody flew to the parking lot with Marlie quick on her heels. Ready for a fight, Jody was almost disappointed when she saw Laura's car peel away. Tom was nowhere in sight.

"Maybe he rode over with Doug. He brought his folks' car tonight."

"I'm sorry," Jody sighed. "I've just been thinking of myself. I'll change quickly, and we'll meet the guys at the party."

"Great, let's boogie," Marlie said with a laugh. The girls headed back to the auditorium door.

Jody pulled on the door. It didn't budge. "I don't know how to tell you this," she said to Marlie, "but it's locked."

"That's crazy," said Marlie, trying it herself. "Let's try the side doors." They found them locked, too.

"This isn't happening to me," Jody cried. "My party clothes are locked inside."

"There's no one left in there. But don't panic yet, let's check the front door."

It, too, was locked. "There's only one door

left," Marlie said, heading toward the gym. "Keep your fingers crossed."

"Please, please be open," Jody prayed. They both pulled and tugged on the gym door, but it didn't budge. Exasperated, the girls shuffled back to the parking lot.

"Well, that settles it," said Jody. "I'm going to panic now. I can't go to the party dressed like this. Just drop me off at home."

"Don't be ridiculous!" exclaimed Marlie. "You're going to the party."

"I can't go like this," Jody sobbed, opening her coat.

"It doesn't matter what you wear. Besides, it's funky."

"That's easy for you to say. You look terrific."

"Tom won't care about your outfit. He just wants to be with you."

"Yeah, so why didn't he meet me stage left after the show?" Jody was trying hard to control her tears.

"There's only one way to find out," Marlie said sensibly. "Show up at the party and ask him, face to face. We've missed some of the fun by now, anyway. Besides, you don't want Laura to spend any more time with Tom, do you?"

That thought made Jody reconsider. "Why don't you drop me off at home? I'll change and have one of my brothers drive me to the party later."

Ten minutes later, Jody bolted through the back door into the Bauers' family room. "Anybody home?" she yelled.

"Just me," Paul answered. He was watching TV and consuming a large bowl of popcorn.

"After I change my clothes, can you drive me over to the Fieldings' for the cast party?"

"No," Paul said, keeping his eyes on the tube.

"Oh, come on, Paul," Jody pleaded. "I'll do your chores for a week."

"Sorry, no can do."

"Why not? Please, Paul, this is the most important night of my life."

"I would if I could," Paul interrupted. "But Mom and Dad have one of the cars, and Bud's not back from his date yet."

"When's he supposed to get back?" Jody asked as she glanced out the window. Marlie was no longer in the driveway. *Stay calm*, she told herself.

"I don't know."

"I'm going to go upstairs and change," she announced. "If anyone drives up, holler."

"Sure, Jod," Paul said, swinging around in his chair. "Sorry I can't help. How did the show go anyway?"

"Fine until about an hour ago."

Jody ran upstairs and changed into a yellow corduroy shirt dress. As she touched up her face and hair, she watched out the window, hoping for a car to drive up. "It's already eleven o'clock," she said as she returned to the family room to wait. "Where is Bud, anyway?"

Paul looked sympathetic but basically ignored her as Jody tried sitting, pacing, and biting her fingernails. Finally at eleven-thirty Bud pulled into the driveway. Jody grabbed her coat and purse and met him before he had reached the garage. "Can you take me to the cast party?" she asked, jumping into the front seat.

"Sure," Bud said, smiling, "Where's the fire?"

"Fieldings'!" Jody said, squirming into her seat belt. She gave him the address, and Bud took off.

"Can't we go any faster?" Jody demanded three blocks later.

"Not without getting arrested. Relax, five more minutes and we'll be there."

Jody stared out the window and tried to think about the party with Tom. "Finally," she whispered as they turned down Laura's street.

"Which house?" Bud inquired.

"The one on the left with all the cars," Jody said, pointing.

"You mean where all the cars are leaving."

"They can't," she moaned, "not yet."

"Well, what do you want to do?" Bud asked, slowing down. "It looks like the party's over. Everyone is going home."

"This isn't happening to me!" Jody said, holding back the tears.

"I'm sorry, kiddo," Bud said sympathetically.

"Let's go home," Jody said, choking on her words. "What a night. I should have turned around a *billion* times to get rid of all the bad luck I'm having now."

Chapter Twelve

"I'm mad at you," Marlie announced in Jody's bedroom the next afternoon. "Why didn't you come to the party?"

"I tried, but everyone was leaving when I got there." Jody, dressed in Bud's sweatshirt, was sitting on her bed.

"Tom looked really disappointed. I should have made you go the way you were dressed."

"It's all right, Marlie, there'll be other parties. We still have closing night next week. I've gotten over it now." Jody crossed her legs Indian-style and rested her elbows on her knees. "So tell me all about it. What did you do? What did Tom do? I want every detail."

"I shouldn't tell you anything," Marlie said, lying down on the floor and putting her feet up on the bed.

"Come on." Jody slapped Marlie's right foot.

"Okay, okay. Tom played Ping-Pong most of the night. He even beat Jeff."

"Justice lives," Jody cheered.

"And when he wasn't playing Ping-Pong, he was either standing by the front door or asking me when you were going to get there."

"I'm sorry, Marls."

"It's okay. Doug and I watched some videos, ate hamburgers, and sang around the piano."

"Sounds like you had fun."

"You should have seen Laura."

"Of course, she looked great."

"Of course, but she was flirting around like it was the Academy Awards. She acted ridiculous, calling everyone 'darling.' "

"Always the center of attention."

"Jeff was worse," Marlie said, standing up to imitate him. "He stood next to the piano, singing at the top of his lungs."

"What a show-off."

"Well, they make the perfect couple. Perfect for what I don't know— Look, I just came by to give you a hard time," Marlie said. "I'm running some errands for my mom. You want to come with me?"

"Thanks, anyway," Jody said. "But I'll walk you to your car. Marlie, Tom didn't say he was mad, did he?"

"No, he just looked a little lost. I think he was debating whether or not to call you, but he was afraid he might wake your folks up. I'll bet he calls today."

"I hope so," Jody said, "but at least I can see him tonight." They walked outside. "Thanks for coming by."

"See you tonight."

"Sure thing," Jody said, waving. *What a beautiful day*, she thought, looking at the light blue sky. She took a deep breath and gazed toward the field where she and Tom had picked the dried flowers. *What a great day that was*, she thought, strolling past the cottonwood trees.

It felt good to be outside walking, so she snapped up the rest of her jacket and kept going past the milkweed stalks and the faded pussy willows. Jody was smiling as she relived each moment. She walked up the hill where she had clung to the handlebars for dear life and laughed as she skipped down the street past the orthodontist's office.

Jody's hands were getting cold so she gave them a quick rub and stuck them in the pockets of her jean jacket. She wasn't ready to go home yet, so she kept walking, thinking about Tom. It was strange, but now that the show had opened, they wouldn't see each other as much. There was the show that night, but then no more daily rehearsals. They wouldn't see each other until next Thursday when they had a brush up rehearsal before the closing weekend. *I wish it weren't going to be over,* Jody thought. *What will happen then? Surely he'll remember saying we'd get together after he got his driver's license. Marlie and Doug are going steady, and we haven't even kissed! Each time we've gotten close, something keeps it from happening.*

Jody glanced at her watch and couldn't believe it was four o'clock. *I've got to get home,* she realized. She'd been so absorbed in her thoughts that she hadn't even noticed the snow flakes that were gently beginning to fall. She pulled her collar up against the cold and jogged home.

Jody sauntered up the front walk and noticed something leaning against the door. She unwrapped a small bundle of fresh daisies and opened the envelope with her name on it. Inside was a note written on blue construction paper.

Jody—
   I really missed you at the party last night. I'm sorry you didn't come. I was hoping to make up for not meeting you backstage as

we planned. I got locked out! Let's try again tonight, same place, five minutes before the show starts.

Forgive me,

Tom

Jody held the note closely to her heart and smelled the flowers. Gently, she turned the handle on the door and walked inside.

"I was starting to worry about you," Mrs. Bauer said as Jody came through the back door.

"Can you believe the snow?" Jody said shaking off her wet jacket. "I hadn't planned to walk so long."

"Well, you can take a hot bath and eat something before you go over to school."

"Thanks, Mom," Jody said smiling.

"Pretty flowers," Mrs. Bauer said. "From anyone special?"

"A secret admirer," Jody answered, placing the daisies in water.

Just as she was ready to go upstairs the phone rang.

"Hello," Jody answered.

"Jody"—Mrs. French's usually calm voice sounded tense—"I just got a call from Mrs. Reynolds, and she said Jeff has lost his voice."

"Lost his voice!" Jody exclaimed. "How did that happen?"

"Well, it seems that he sang too loudly and too long at the party last night and woke up with not much of a voice. He'd hoped it would get better by this afternoon, but his mother says he still sounds squeaky."

"What are we going to do?" Jody asked.

"I found a replacement, and we're over at the school rehearsing now. Come over as soon as possible, and we'll try to work through some of your dance numbers."

"Okay," Jody answered, a little confused. "I'll take a quick shower and be right over."

She hung up the phone and started scurrying around the kitchen.

"What's going on?" Mrs. Bauer asked. "You look like a chicken with its head chopped off."

"Jeff's lost his voice," Jody mumbled, trying to eat an apple. "So they have a replacement, and they're rehearsing now."

"Who is it?"

"I don't know. Mrs. French didn't say," Jody shouted over her shoulder, bounding up the stairs three at a time.

"Can I do anything to help?" her mother called after her.

"If you could take me over to school after my shower, that would save some time."

"Whenever you're ready."

"Thanks, Mom, you're the best," Jody cried as she disappeared into the bathroom.

She rushed her shower, threw on enough makeup to give herself a head start before the show, and swept her damp hair on top of her head into a twist. Then she stormed downstairs, snatching her wool coat and scarf.

"Ready when you are, Mom," Jody called as she grabbed a soda from the refrigerator.

"Do you have everything you need?" Mrs. Bauer asked as they rolled out of the driveway. "If you think of anything, just call and we'll bring it with us when we come tonight."

Jody smiled at her mother. She was glad her family was coming to the performance that night.

"I think I have everything," said Jody, biting her nails.

"And remember, no matter what happens tonight we're proud of you. So enjoy yourself and have fun."

"Thanks, Mom," Jody said, hopping out of the car.

She pushed open the front door and rushed to the auditorium entrance. As her eyes adjusted to the dark arena, she carefully walked to the side of the stage. Mrs. French was giving some final instructions to Jeff's replacement.

"I hope I don't forget these dance steps," Tom said to Jody as she walked center stage.

"You're Jeff's replacement?" she cried, her mouth falling open.

"Are you sorry?" Tom asked quietly.

"Are you kidding?" Jody answered, taking his hands. "I just can't believe it!"

"Let's start with the first dance combination," Mrs. French interrupted. "Have you watched the number before, Tom?"

"Every day," he answered, his eyes focused on Jody.

"Let's give it a try, then," Mrs. French said, nodding to the accompanist.

Tom followed Jody's lead and they went through the dance with only a few mistakes.

"Fine," Mrs. French said, smiling. "Go over it again backstage and practice the second-act numbers during the first-act intermission. But now, Tom, we need to see how the costumes fit."

In her excitement, Jody hadn't realized that she'd been clutching Tom's hand, almost cutting off his circulation.

"Ooh," Jody said, letting go slowly. "I guess I'm nervous, too."

"I'm not worried," Tom whispered. "The audience will still be watching you."

"I doubt it," Jody said, thinking he'd never

looked so handsome. She was sure every girl in the audience would be watching Tom.

"You're needed in the dressing room now, Tom," Mrs. French called from stage left.

"I'd better go," Tom said, gazing into Jody's eyes. "I'll meet you backstage."

"And *onstage*," Jody answered, smiling.

Once again the cast joined hands in the green room for that evening's pep talk. But there was a new electricity in the air, an exciting energy that Jody felt as she and Tom once again clasped hands. *Everything feels right*, Jody thought, *Tom is doing the lead, and we'll be onstage together*. A quick wish and it was time to go to "places" and the start of the show.

As soon as Jody and Tom stepped onto the stage for their first scene, Jody felt the magic begin. The way they felt about each other offstage came alive with each note Tom sang and every step Jody took. It all worked together perfectly. Jody couldn't believe how quickly the show was going. She wanted to hold on to each passing moment to make it last a little longer. She knew Jeff would be back the next weekend, so she made mental pictures of everything she and Tom were doing now. Jody paused before her entrance for the love scene and thought how nice it was that her family was seeing *this* performance. Somehow that made it all the more special.

Here I go, she thought with a sigh as she ran onstage for the love scene with Tom.

It feels different, she thought as they began their parts. It was as if all the words and emotions they felt offstage were culminating during this scene. Jody danced her feelings for Tom through her character of Susan:

I feel all fuzzy when I'm with you, her steps explained.

"I feel the same frenzy when I'm with you," Tom's character, Og, answered.

Jody hugged him, and their eyes met.

"Is this what it's like to be mortal?" Tom's leprechaun character asked gleefully.

Jody nodded and nuzzled closer. She wished she were brave enough to do this offstage, but finally she was sure that Tom knew how she felt. There was an unmistakable electricity between them.

The dance went smoothly, miraculously without mistakes. Jody kept thinking how much fun it all was. Dancing had never felt so wonderful; it was as if she were soaring across the stage. Jody got so carried away by the steps, she forgot about the kiss that was to follow.

The dance ended, and the applause faded. Tom gazed down at Jody. He took his right hand and slowly raised her chin upward. As Jody closed her eyes, all her senses heightened. The crowd was silent. She could hear her heart beat in rhythm with Tom's. Then suddenly as if a soft, summer breeze swept across her mouth, Jody felt Tom's gentle, warm lips meet hers. *This is heaven*, she thought. Tom pulled back for a moment and Jody tried to catch her breath.

"That was for the show," he whispered. "This one's from me." Then even more tenderly than the first, Tom kissed her again. Jody knew then without a doubt that this moment would last forever.

SATIN SLIPPERS

by Elizabeth Bernard

Available wherever Bantam paperbacks are sold!

It is many young girls' dream to become a ballerina, to step into pink satin toe shoes, pirouette in the spotlight, dance the solo of the Sugar Plum Fairy . . . and curtsy to a thunderous applause in a packed auditorium.

It is certainly fifteen-year-old Leah Stephenson's dream. For ten years she has practiced, trained and hoped for nothing else.

Live through all the joys and heartaches of becoming a ballerina with Leah and her friends in the SATIN SLIPPERS series.

1 TO BE A DANCER
2 CENTRE STAGE
3 STARS IN HER EYES
4 CHANGING PARTNERS

SILVER SKATES

by Barbara J. Mumma

To become a top figure skater you need talent, determination and dedication. Just as important however, as four young hopefuls Claire, Whitney, Cindi and Katie find out, are good friends!

Coming soon from wherever Bantam paperbacks are sold:

1 BREAKING THE ICE
2 WINNER'S WALTZ
3 FACE THE MUSIC
4 TWO TO TANGO